TALES OF TOWN
& COUNTRY

ABOUT THE AUTHOR

Willa Sibert Cather (1873–1947) is best known for her trilogy of novels of frontier life: *O Pioneers!* (1913), *The Song of the Lark* (1915), and *My Ántonia* (1918). But she was a prolific short-story writer as well, and her stories explored not only the harshness of immigrant life on the prairie but also the sophisticated and artistic city life of the East.

Cather was born in Virginia and moved at the age of nine to Nebraska, where her father briefly farmed and later was a businessman. Cather began publishing stories and articles as a girl in local papers like the *Red Cloud Chief*, the *Nebraska State Journal*, the *Lincoln Courier*, and *The Hesperian*, the campus newspaper at the University of Nebraska, where she was a student.

In her early twenties, Cather moved to Pittsburgh, where she taught high school, wrote journalism for the *Pittsburgh Leader*, and contributed poetry and short fiction to periodicals. In 1906 she moved to New York to become an editor for *McClure's Magazine*.

Cather's novels, particularly her prairie trilogy and *Death Comes for the Archbishop* (1927), were critical as well as commercial successes. She was awarded the Pulitzer Prize in 1922 and the gold medal of the National Institute of Arts and Letters in 1944. During Cather's lifetime, J. B. Priestley called her America's greatest novelist, and in our own time A. S. Byatt has commented on "the fierceness and power of her writing."

TALES OF TOWN & COUNTRY

Willa Cather

RUSHWATER PRESS

P.O. Box 50151
Sarasota, FL 34232, USA

Includes editors' note and biographical sketch.

PUBLISHER'S CATALOGING-IN-PUBLICATION DATA
Names: Cather, Willa, 1873–1947.
Title: Tales of town and country / Willa Cather.
Description: Sarasota, FL: Rushwater Press, 2017
Identifiers: ISBN 978-0-9801532-2-4
Subjects: LCSH United States—Social life and customs—
20th century—Fiction. | Women immigrants—Fiction. |
Women pioneers—Fiction. | Farm life—Fiction. |
New York (N.Y.)—History—Fiction. | Short stories, American. | BISAC
FICTION / Short Stories (single author)
Classification: LCC PS3505.A87 .T35 2017 | DDC 813/.52—dc23

Printed in the United States of America
www.rushwaterpress.com
10 9 8 7 6 5 4 3 2 1

FIRST EDITION

Book design by Simon M. Sullivan

Cover illustration by Shutterstock.
Author photo courtesy of the Nebraska State Historical Society.

———

These seven stories by Willa Cather, edited by Patricia T. O'Conner and Stewart Kellerman for Rushwater Press, are published here under the title *Tales of Town & Country*. All but one first appeared in periodicals.

"A Death in the Desert" originally appeared in *Scribner's Magazine*, January 1903.

"The Bohemian Girl" was first published *McClure's Magazine*, August 1912.

"A Gold Slipper" originally appeared in *Harper's Monthly Magazine*, January 1917.

"On the Divide" was first printed in *Overland Monthly*, January 1896.

"Flavia and Her Artists" originally appeared in a collection of Cather's stories, *The Troll Garden*, published in March 1905 by McClure, Phillips & Co.

"The Bookkeeper's Wife" first appeared in *The Century Illustrated Monthly Magazine*, May 1916.

"Her Boss" was first published in October 1919 in both the American and the British editions of the magazine *Smart Set*. The version included here is from the American edition.

CONTENTS

A DEATH IN THE DESERT

WINDERMERE HILGARDE was conscious that the man in the seat across the aisle was looking at him intently. He was a large, florid man, wore a conspicuous diamond solitaire upon his third finger, and Windermere judged him to be a travelling salesman of some sort. He had the air of an adaptable fellow who had been about the world and who could keep cool and clean under almost any circumstances.

The "High Line Flyer," as this train was derisively called among railroad men, was jerking along through the hot afternoon over the monotonous country between Holdredge and Cheyenne. Besides the blond man and himself the only occupants of the car were two dusty, bedraggled-looking girls who had been to the Exposition at Chicago, and who were earnestly discussing the cost of their first trip out of Colorado. The four uncomfortable passengers were covered with a sediment of fine, yellow dust which clung to their hair and eyebrows like gold powder. It blew up in clouds from the bleak, lifeless country through which they passed, until they were one color with the sage-brush and sand-hills. The gray and yellow desert was varied only by occasional ruins of deserted towns, and the little red boxes of station-houses, where the spindling trees and sickly vines in the blue-grass yards were kept alive only by continual hypodermic injections of water from the tank where the engines were watered, little green reserves fenced off in that confusing wilderness of sand.

As the slanting rays of the sun beat in stronger and stronger through the car-windows, the blond gentleman asked the ladies' permission to remove his coat, and sat in his lavender striped shirt-sleeves, with a black silk handkerchief tucked carefully about his collar. He had seemed interested in Windermere since they had boarded the train at Holdredge, and kept glancing at him curiously and then looking reflectively out of the window, as though he were trying to recall something. But wherever Windermere went someone was almost sure to look at him with that curious interest, and it had ceased to embarrass or annoy him. Presently the stranger, seeming satisfied with his observation, leaned back in his seat, half closed his eyes, and began softly to whistle the Spring Song from "Proserpine," the cantata that a dozen years before had made its young composer famous in a night. Windermere had heard that air on guitars in Old Mexico, on mandolins at college glees, on cottage organs in New England hamlets, and only two weeks ago he had heard it played on sleighbells at a variety theatre in Denver. There was literally no way of escaping his brother's precocity. Adriance could live on the other side of the Atlantic, where his youthful indiscretions were forgotten in his mature achievements, but his brother had never been able to outrun "Proserpine," and here he found it again in the Colorado sand-hills. Not that Windermere was exactly ashamed of "Proserpine"; only a man of genius could have written it, but it was the sort of thing that a man of genius outgrows as soon as he can, and its popularity was the gravest charge conservative critics could make against it.

Windermere unbent a trifle, and smiled at his neighbor across the aisle. Immediately the large man rose and coming over dropped into the seat facing Hilgarde, extending his card.

"Dusty ride, isn't it? I don't mind it myself; I'm used to it. Born and bred in de briar patch, like Br'er Rabbit. I've been trying to place you for a long time; I think I must have met you before."

"Thank you," said Windermere, taking the card; "my name is Hilgarde. You've probably met my brother, Adriance; people often mistake me for him."

The travelling-man brought his hand down upon his knee with such vehemence that the solitaire blazed.

"So I was right after all, and if you're not Adriance Hilgarde you're his double. I thought I couldn't be mistaken. Seen him? Well, I guess! I never missed one of his recitals at the Auditorium, and he played the piano score of 'Proserpine' through to us once at the Chicago Press Club. I used to be on the *Commercial* there before I began to travel for the publishing department of the concern. So you're Hilgarde's brother, and here I've run into you at the jumping-off place. Sounds like a newspaper yarn, doesn't it?"

The travelling-man laughed and offered Windermere a cigar and plied him with questions on the only subject that people ever seemed to care to talk to Windermere about. At length the salesman and the two girls alighted at a Colorado way station, and Windermere went on to Cheyenne alone.

The train pulled into Cheyenne at nine o'clock, late by a matter of four hours or so; but no one seemed particularly concerned at its tardiness except the station agent, who grumbled at being kept in the office over time on a summer night. When Windermere alighted from the train he walked down the platform and stopped at the track crossing, uncertain as to what direction he should take to reach a hotel. A phaëton stood near the crossing and a woman held the reins. She was dressed in white and her figure was clearly silhouetted against the cushions, though it was too dark to see her face. Windermere had scarcely noticed her, when the switch-engine came puffing up from the opposite direction, and the head-light threw a strong glare of light on his face. Suddenly the woman in the phaëton uttered a low cry and dropped the reins. Windermere started forward and caught the horse's head, but the animal only lifted its ears and whisked its tail in impatient surprise. The woman sat perfectly still, her head sunk between her shoulders and her handkerchief pressed to her face. Another woman came out of the depot and hurried toward the phaëton, crying, "Katharine, dear, what is the matter?"

Windermere hesitated a moment in painful embarrassment, then lifted his hat and passed on. He was accustomed to sudden recognitions in the most impossible places, especially by women, but this cry out of the night had shaken him.

While Windermere was breakfasting the next morning, the head waiter leaned over his chair to murmur that there was a gentleman waiting to see him in the parlor. Windermere finished his coffee, and went in the direction indicated, where he found his visitor restlessly pacing the floor. His whole manner betrayed a high degree of nervous agitation, though his physique was not that of a man whose nerves lie near the surface. He was something below medium height, square-shouldered and solidly built. His thick, closely cut hair was beginning to show gray about the ears, and his bronzed face was heavily lined. His square brown hands were locked behind him, and he held his shoulders like a man conscious of responsibilities, yet, as he turned to greet Windermere, there was an incongruous diffidence in his address.

"Good-morning, Mr. Hilgarde," he said, extending his hand; "I found your name on the hotel register. My name is Gaylord; I'm afraid my sister startled you at the station last night, Mr. Hilgarde, and I've come around to apologize."

"Ah! the young lady in the phaëton? I'm sure I didn't know whether I had anything to do with her alarm or not. If I did, it is I who owe the apology, and I make it to you most sincerely."

The man colored a little under the dark brown on his face.

"Oh, it's nothing you could help, sir, I fully understand that. You see, my sister used to be a pupil of your brother's, and it seems you favor him, and when the switch-engine threw a light on your face it startled her."

Windermere wheeled about in his chair. "Oh! *Katharine* Gaylord! Is it possible! Now it's you who have given me a turn. Why, I used to know her when I was a boy. What on earth—"

"Is she doing here?" said Gaylord, grimly filling out the

pause. "You've got at the heart of the matter. You knew my sister had been in bad health for a long time?"

"No, I had never heard a word of that. The last I knew of her she was singing in London. My brother and I correspond infrequently, and seldom get beyond family matters. I am deeply sorry to hear this. There are many reasons why I should be more concerned than I can tell you."

The lines in Charley Gaylord's brow relaxed a little.

"What I'm trying to say, Mr. Hilgarde, is that she wants to see you. I hate to ask you, but she's so set on it. We live several miles out of town, but my rig's below, and I can take you out any time you can go."

"I can go now, and it will give me real pleasure to do so," said Windermere, quickly. "I'll get my hat and be with you in a moment."

When he came downstairs Windermere found a cart at the door, and Charley Gaylord drew a long sigh of relief as he gathered up the reins and settled back into his own element.

"You see, I think I'd better tell you something about my sister before you see her, and I don't know just where to begin. She travelled in Europe with your brother and his wife, and sang at a lot of his concerts; but I don't know just how much you know about her."

"Very little, except that my brother always thought her the most gifted of his pupils, and that when I knew her she was very young and very beautiful and turned my head sadly for a while."

Windermere saw that Gaylord's mind was quite engrossed by his grief. He was wrought up to the point where his reserve and sense of proportion had quite left him, and his trouble was the one vital thing in the world. "That's the whole thing," he went on, flecking his horses with the whip.

"She was a great woman, as you say, and she didn't come of a great family. She had to fight her own way from the first. She got to Chicago, and then to New York, and then to Europe, where she went up like lightning, and got a taste for it all, and now she's dying here like a rat in a hole, out of her own world, and she can't fall back into ours. We've grown apart, someway—miles and miles apart— and I'm afraid she's fearfully unhappy."

"It's a very tragic story that you are telling, Gaylord," said Windermere. They were well out into the country now, spinning along over the dusty plains of red grass, with the ragged blue outline of the mountains before them.

"Tragic!" cried Gaylord, starting up in his seat, "my God, man, nobody will ever know how tragic. It's a tragedy I live with and eat with and sleep with, until I've lost my grip on everything. You see she had made a good bit of money, but she spent it all going to health resorts. It's her lungs, you know. I've got money enough to send her anywhere, but the doctors all say it's no use. She hasn't the ghost of a chance. It's just getting through the days until the end now. I had no notion she was half so bad before she came to me. She just wrote that she was all run down. Now that she's here, I think she'd be happier anywhere under the sun, but she won't leave. She says it's easier to let go of life here, and that to go East would be dying twice. There was a time when I was a brakeman with a run out of Bird City, Iowa, and she was a little thing I could carry on my shoulder, when I could get her everything on earth she wanted, and she hadn't a wish my $80 a month didn't cover; and now, when I've got a little property together, I can't buy her a night's sleep!" He stopped with a gulp and half closed his eyes.

Windermere saw that, whatever Charley Gaylord's present status in the world might be, he had brought the brakeman's heart up the ladder with him, and the brakeman's frank avowal of sentiment. Presently Gaylord went on:

"You can understand how she has outgrown her family. We're all a pretty common sort, railroaders from away back. My father was a conductor. He died when we were kids. Maggie, my other sister, who lives with me, was a telegraph operator here while I was getting my grip on things. We had no education to speak of. I have to hire a stenographer because I can't spell straight—the Almighty couldn't teach me to spell. The things that make up life to Kate are all Greek to me, and there's scarcely a point where we touch any more, except in our recollections of the old times when we were all young and happy together, and Kate sang in a church choir in Bird City. But I believe, Mr. Hilgarde, that if she can see just one person like you, who knows about the things and people she cares for, it will give her about the only comfort she can have now."

The reins slackened in Charley Gaylord's hand as they drew up before a showily painted house with many gables and a round tower. "Here we are," he said, turning to Windermere, "and I guess we understand each other."

They were met at the door by a thin, colorless woman,

whom Gaylord introduced as "My sister, Maggie." She asked her brother to show Mr. Hilgarde into the music-room, where Katharine wished to see him alone.

When Windermere entered the music-room he gave a little start of surprise, feeling that he had stepped from the glaring Wyoming sunlight into some New York studio that he had always known. He wondered which it was of those countless studios, high up under the roofs, over banks and shops and wholesale houses, that this room resembled, and he looked incredulously out of the window at the gray plain that ended in the great upheaval of the Rockies. There are little skeleton-closets of the arts scattered here and there all over the West, where some Might-Have-Been hides his memories and the trophies of his student days on the Continent and the rusty tools of the craft that he once believed had called him; but this room savored of the present, and about it there was an air of immediate touch with the art of the present.

On the walls were autograph sketches by several of the younger American painters, and young Scotchmen whose names were scarcely known on this side of the water. Above one of the book-cases was a large photograph of Rodin's Balzac; on the music-rack were the scores of Massenet's latest opera and Chaminade's latest song. It seemed scarcely possible that the glad tidings of these things should have reached Wyoming already. The haunting air of familiarity about the place perplexed Windermere. Was the room a copy of some particular studio he knew, or was it merely the studio atmosphere that seemed so individual and poignantly reminiscent here in Wyoming? He sat down in a reading-chair and looked keenly about him. Suddenly his eye fell upon a large photograph of his brother, framed in dark wood, above the piano. Then it all became clear to him: this was veritably his brother's room. If it were not an exact copy of one of the many studios that Adriance had fitted up in various parts of the world, wearying of them and leaving almost before the renovator's varnish had dried, it was at least in the same tone. In every detail Adriance's taste was so manifest that the room seemed to exhale his personality. The black oak ceiling and floor, the dull red walls, the huge brick fire-place with a Wagnerian inscription on the tiles, the old Venetian lamp that hung under the copy of the Mona Lisa, the cast of the Parthenon frieze that ran about the room, the tall brass candlesticks with their sacerdotal candles, were all exactly as Adriance would have had them.

Among the photographs on the wall there was one of Katharine Gaylord, taken in the days when Windermere had known her and when the flash of her eye or the flutter of her skirt was enough to set his boyish heart in a tumult. Even now, he stood before the portrait with a certain degree of embarrassment. It was the face of a woman already old in her first youth, thoroughly sophisticated and a trifle hard, and it told of what her brother had called her fight. The *camaraderie* of her frank, confident eyes was qualified by the deep lines about her mouth and the curve of the lips, which was both sad and cynical. Certainly she had more good-will than confidence toward the world, and the bravado of her smile could not conceal the shadow of an unrest that was almost discontent. Perhaps that, too, was only the scar of the struggle of which her brother had spoken; perhaps the long warfare against adverse conditions had brought about an almost antagonistic and distrustful attitude of mind. The chief charm of the woman, as Windermere had known her, lay in her superb figure and in her eyes, which possessed a warm, life-giving quality like the sunlight; generous, fearless eyes, which glowed with sympathy and good-cheer for all living things, a sort of perpetual *salutat* to the world. Her head Windermere remembered as peculiarly well shaped and proudly poised. There had been always a little of the imperatrix about her, and her pose in the photograph revived all his old impressions of her unattachedness, of how absolutely and valiantly she stood alone.

Windermere was still standing before the picture, his hands behind him and his head inclined, when he heard the door open. A very tall woman advanced toward him, holding out her hand. As she started to speak she coughed slightly, then, laughing, said, in a low, rich voice, a trifle husky: "You see I make the traditional Camille entrance—with the cough. How good of you to come, Mr. Hilgarde."

Windermere was acutely conscious that while addressing him she was not looking at him at all, and, as he assured her of his pleasure in coming, he was glad to have an opportunity to collect himself. He had not reckoned on the ravages of a long illness. The long, loose folds of her white gown had been especially designed to disguise the sharp outlines of her emaciated body, but the stamp of her disease was there, simple and ugly and obtrusive, a pitiless fact that could not be disguised nor evaded. The splendid shoulders were stooped, there was a swaying unevenness in her gait, her arms seemed disproportionately long, and her hands were transparently white and cold to the touch as water-flowers. Her chest, that full, proud singer's chest, that had swelled like the bellows of an organ when she took her high notes, was fallen and flat. The changes in her face were less obvious; the proud carriage of the head, the warm, clear eyes, even the delicate flush of color in her cheeks, all defiantly remained, though they were all in a lower key—older, sadder, softer.

She sat down upon the divan and began nervously arranging the pillows. "I know I'm not an inspiring object to look upon, but you must be quite frank and sensible about that and get used to it at once, for we've no time to lose. And if I'm a trifle irritable you won't mind?—for I'm more than usually nervous."

"Don't bother with me this morning if you are tired," urged Windermere. "I can come quite as well to-morrow."

"Gracious, no!" she protested, with a flash of that quick, keen humor that he remembered as a part of her. "It's solitude that I'm tired to death of, solitude and the wrong kind of people. You see, the minister, not content with reading the prayers for the sick, called on me this morning. He happened to be riding by on his bicycle and felt it his duty to stop. Of course, he disapproves of my profession, and I think he takes it for granted that I have a dark past. The funniest feature of his conversation is that he is always excusing my own vocation to me—condoning it, you know—and trying to patch up my peace with my conscience by suggesting possible noble uses for what he kindly calls my talent."

Windermere laughed. "Oh! I'm afraid I'm not the person to call after such a serious gentleman—I can't sustain the situation. At my best—I don't reach higher than low comedy. Have you decided to which one of the noble uses you will devote yourself?"

Katharine lifted her hands in a gesture of renunciation and went on: "I'm not equal to any of them, not even the least noble. I didn't study that method. Neither Marchesi nor your brother taught me the moral purpose of singing the scales."

Katharine laughed indulgently. "The parson's not so bad. His English never offends me, and he has read Gibbon's 'Decline and Fall,' all five volumes, and that's something. Then, he has been to New York, and that's a great deal. But how we are losing time! Do tell me about New York; Charley says you're just on from there. How does it look and taste and smell just now? I think a whiff of the Jersey ferry would be as flagons of cod-liver oil to me. Who conspicuously walks the Rialto now, and what does he or she wear? Are the trees still green in Madison Square, or have they grown brown and dusty? Does the chaste Diana on the Garden Theatre still keep her vestal vows through all the exasperating changes of weather? Who has your brother's old studio now, and what misguided aspirants practise their scales in the rookeries above Carnegie Hall? What do people go to see at the theatres, and what do they eat and drink there in the world nowadays? You see, I love it all,

from the Battery to Riverside. Oh, let me die in Harlem!"
She was interrupted by a violent attack of coughing, and
Windermere, embarrassed by her discomfort, plunged into
gossip about the professional people he had met in town
during the summer, and the musical outlook for the winter. He was diagramming with his pencil, on the back of an
old envelope he found in his pocket, some new mechanical
device to be used at the Metropolitan in the production of
the "Rheingold," when he became conscious that she was
looking at him intently, and that he was talking to the four
walls.

Katharine was lying back among the pillows, watching
him through half-closed eyes, as a painter looks at a picture. He finished his explanation vaguely enough and put
the envelope back in his pocket. As he did so, she said,
quietly: "How wonderfully like Adriance you are!" and he
felt as though a crisis of some sort had been met and tided
over.

He laughed, looking up at her with a touch of pride in
his eyes that made them seem quite boyish. "Yes, isn't it
absurd? It's almost as awkward as looking like Napoleon—
there's no possibility of living up to the part. I really believe
it kept me out of a scrape or two when I was in college,
and, after all, there are some advantages. It has made some
of his friends like me, and I hope it will make you."

Katharine smiled and gave him a quick, meaning glance
from under her lashes. "Oh, it did that long ago. What a
haughty, reserved youth you were then, and how you used
to stare at people, and then blush and look cross if they
paid you back in your own coin. Do you remember that

night when you took me home from a rehearsal and scarcely spoke a word to me?"

"It was the silence of admiration," protested Windermere, "very crude and boyish, but very sincere and not a little painful. Perhaps you suspected something of the sort? I remember you saw fit to be very grown up and worldly."

"I believe I suspected a pose; the one that college boys usually affect with singers—'an earthen vessel in love with a star,' you know. But it rather surprised me in you, for you must have seen a good deal of your brother's pupils. Or had you an omnivorous capacity, and elasticity that always met the occasion?"

"Don't ask a man to confess the follies of his youth," said Windermere, smiling a little sadly; "I am sensitive about some of them even now. But I was not so sophisticated as you imagined. I saw my brother's pupils come and go, but that was about all. Sometimes I was called on to play accompaniments, or to fill out a vacancy at a rehearsal, or to order a carriage for an infuriated soprano who had thrown up her part, but they never spent any time on me, unless it was to notice the resemblance you speak of."

"Yes," observed Katharine, thoughtfully, "I noticed it then, too, but it has grown as you have grown older. That is rather strange, when you have lived such different lives. It's not merely an ordinary family likeness of feature, you know, but a sort of interchangeable individuality, the suggestion of the other man's personality in your face, like an air transposed to another key. But I'm not attempting to define it; it's beyond me, something altogether unusual and a trifle—well, uncanny," she finished, laughing.

"I remember," Windermere said, seriously, twirling the pencil between his fingers and looking, as he sat with his head thrown back, out under the red window-blind which was raised just a little, and as it swung back and forth in the wind revealed the glaring panorama of the desert, a blinding stretch of yellow, flat as the sea in dead calm, splotched here and there with deep purple shadows, and, beyond, the ragged blue outline of the mountains and the peaks of snow, white as the white clouds—"I remember, when I was a little fellow I used to be very sensitive about it. I don't think it exactly displeased me, or that I would have had it otherwise if I could, but it seemed to me like a birthmark, or something not to be lightly spoken of. People were naturally always fonder of Ad than of me, and I used to feel the chill of reflected light pretty often. It affected even my relations with my mother. Ad went abroad to study when he was absurdly young, you know, and mother was all broken up over it. She did her whole duty by each of us, but it was sort of generally understood among us that she'd have made burnt-offerings of us all for Ad any day. I was a little fellow then, and when she sat alone on the porch in the summer dusk, she used sometimes to call me to her and turn my face up in the light that streamed out through the shutters and kiss me, and then I always knew she was thinking of Adriance."

"Poor little chap," said Katharine, and her tone was a trifle huskier than usual. "How fond people have always been of Adriance! Now tell me the latest news of him. I haven't heard, except through the press, for a year or more. He was in Algiers then, in the valley of the Chelif, riding horseback night and day in an Arabian costume, and in his usual enthusiastic fashion he had quite made up his mind to adopt the Mahometan faith and become as nearly an Arab as possible. How many countries and faiths has he adopted, I wonder? Probably he was playing Arab to himself all the time. I remember he was a sixteenth-century duke in Florence once for weeks together."

"Oh, that's Adriance," chuckled Windermere. "He is himself barely long enough to write checks and be measured for his clothes. I didn't hear from him while he was an Arab; I missed that."

"Well, he had a piano carted out into the desert somehow, and was living in a tent beside a dried water-course grown up with dwarf oleanders. He was writing an Algerian *suite* for the piano then; it must be in the publisher's hands by this time. I have been too ill to answer his letter, and have lost touch with him."

Windermere drew a letter from his pocket. "This came about a month ago. It's chiefly about his new opera which is to be brought out in London next winter. Read it at your leisure."

"I think I shall keep it as a hostage, so that I may be sure you will come again. Now I want you to play for me. Whatever you like; but if there is anything new in the world, in mercy let me hear it. For nine months I have heard nothing but 'The Baggage Coach Ahead' and 'She is My Baby's Mother.' "

He sat down at the piano, and Katharine sat near him, absorbed in his remarkable physical likeness to his brother, and trying to discover in just what it consisted. Windermere was not even a handsome man, and everyone admitted that his brother was. Katharine told herself that it was very much as though a sculptor's finished work had been rudely copied in wood. He was of a larger build than Adriance, and his shoulders were broad and heavy, while those of his brother were slender and rather girlish. His face was of the same oval mould, but it was gray, and darkened about the mouth by continual shaving. His eyes were of the same inconstant April color, but they were reflective and rather dull, while Adriance's were always points of high light, and always meaning another thing than the thing they meant yesterday. But it was hard to see why this earnest man should so continually suggest that lyric, youthful face that was as gay as his was grave. For Adriance, though he was ten years older, and though his hair was streaked with silver, had the face of a boy of twenty, so mobile that it told his thoughts before he could put them into words or music, and responded to the nerve-centres of his sensitive brain as the keyboard to the touch. A contralto, famous for the extravagance of her vocal methods and of her affections, had once said of him that the shepherd-boys who sang under the oaks in the Vale of Tempe must certainly have looked like young Hilgarde, and the comparison had been appropriated by a hundred shyer women who preferred to quote.

As Windermere sat smoking on the veranda of the Inter-Ocean House that night, he was a victim to random recollections. His infatuation for Katharine Gaylord, visionary as it was, had been the most serious of his boyish love-affairs, and had long disturbed his bachelor dreams. He was painfully timid in everything relating to the emotions, and his hurt had withdrawn him from the society of women. The fact that it was all so done and dead and far behind him and that the woman had lived her life out since then, gave him an oppressive sense of age and loss. He bethought himself of something that Stevenson had said about sitting by the hearth and remembering the faces of women without desire, and felt himself an octogenarian.

He remembered how bitter and morose he had grown during his stay at his brother's studio when Katharine Gaylord was working there, and how he had wounded Adriance on the night of his last concert in New York. He had sat there in the box while his brother and Katharine were called back again and again after the last number, watching the roses go up over the footlights until they were stacked half as high as the piano, brooding, in his sullen boy's heart, upon the pride those two felt in each other's work, spurring each other to their best and beautifully contending in song, as he had read in some Greek lyric. The footlights had seemed a hard, glittering line drawn sharply between their life and his, a circle of flame set about those splendid children of genius. He walked back to his hotel alone, and sat in his window staring out on Madison Square until long after midnight, resolving to beat no more at doors that he could never enter, and realizing more keenly than ever before how far this glorious dream world of production and beautiful creations lay beyond the prow of the merchant marines. He told himself that he had in common with this woman only the baser uses of life. That sixth sense, the passion for perfect expression, and the lustre of her achievement were like a rosy mist veiling her, such as the goddesses of the elder days wrapped about themselves when they vanished from the arms of men.

II

Windermere's week in Cheyenne stretched to three, and he saw no prospect of release except through the thing he dreaded. The bright, windy days of the Wyoming autumn passed swiftly as the sands through an hour-glass. Letters and telegrams came urging him to hasten his trip to the coast, but he resolutely postponed his business engagements. The mornings he spent on one of Charley Gaylord's ponies, or fishing in the mountains, and in the evenings he sat in his room writing letters or reading. In the afternoon he was usually at his post of duty. Destiny seems to have very positive notions about the sort of parts we are fitted to play. The scene changes and the compensation varies, but in the end we usually find that we have played the same class of business from first to last. Windermere Hilgarde had been a stop-gap all his life, and whatever career he embarked upon he drifted back always to the same harbor, refused by the high seas, and found himself doing the work of all his several friends and serving every purpose save his own. He remembered going through a looking-glass labyrinth when he was a boy, and trying gallery after gallery, only at every turn to bump his nose against his own face, which, indeed, was not his own, but his brother's. No matter what his mission, east or west, by land or sea, he was sure to find himself employed in his brother's business, one of the tributary lives which helped to swell the shining current of Adriance Hilgarde's. It was not the first time that his duty had been to comfort as best he could one of the broken things his brother's imperious speed had cast aside and forgotten. He made no attempt to analyze the situation or to state it in exact terms, but he felt Katharine Gaylord's need for him, and he accepted it as a commission from his brother to help this woman to die. Day by day he felt her demands on him grow more imperious, her need for him grow more acute and positive, and day by day he felt that in his peculiar relation to her, his own individuality played a smaller part. His power to minister to her comfort, he saw, lay solely in his link with his brother's life. He understood all that his physical resemblance meant to her. He knew that she sat by him always watching for some common trick of gesture, some familiar play of expression, some trick of light and shadow, in which he should seem wholly Adriance. He knew that she lived upon this and that her disease fed upon it; that it sent shudders of remembrance through her and quickened nerves that the grave had already chilled; that all the womanhood in her cried out for this, and that in the exhaustion which followed this turmoil of her dying senses, she slept deep and sweet, and dreamed of youth and art and days in a certain old Florentine garden, and not of bitterness and death.

The question which most perplexed him was, "How much shall I know? How much does she wish me to know?" A few days after his first meeting with Katharine Gaylord, he had cabled his brother to write her. He had merely said that she was mortally ill; he could depend on Adriance to say the right thing—that was a part of his gift. Adriance always said not only the right thing, but the opportune, graceful, exquisite thing. His phrases took the color of the moment and the then present condition, so that they never savored of perfunctory compliment or frequent usage. He always caught the lyric essence of the moment, the poetic effluvium of every situation. Moreover, he usually did the right thing, the opportune, graceful, exquisite thing—except when he did very cruel things—bent upon making people happy when their existence touched his, just as he insisted that his material environment should be beautiful; lavishing upon those near him all the warmth and radiance of his rich nature, all the homage of the poet and troubadour, and, when they were no longer near, forgetting, for that also was a part of Adriance's gift.

Three weeks after Windermere had sent his cable, when he made his daily call at the gayly painted ranch-house, he found Katharine laughing like a school-girl. "Have you ever thought," she said, as he entered the music-room, "how much these séances of ours are like Heine's 'Florentine Nights,' except that I don't give you an opportunity to monopolize the conversation as Heine did?" She held his hand longer than usual as she greeted him, and looked searchingly up into his face. "You are the kindest man living, the kindest," she added, softly.

Windermere's gray face colored faintly as he drew his hand away, for he felt that this time she was looking at him, and not at a whimsical caricature of his brother. "Why, what have I done now?" he asked, lamely. "I can't remember having sent you any stale candy or champagne since yesterday."

She drew a letter with a foreign postmark from between the leaves of a copy of "*Fort comme la Morte*" and held it out, smiling. "You got him to write it. Don't say you didn't, for it came direct, you see, and the last address I gave him was a place in Florida. This deed shall be remembered of you when I am with the just in Paradise. But one thing you did not ask him to do, for you didn't know about it. He has sent me his latest work, a pastoral sonata, the most ambitious thing he has ever done, and you are to play it for me directly, though it looks horribly intricate. But first for the letter; I think you would better read it aloud to me."

Windermere sat down in a low chair facing the window-seat in which she sat with a barricade of pillows behind her, and playing with the lace on her sleeve; he opened the letter, his lashes half-veiling his kind eyes, and saw to his satisfaction that it was a long one, wonderfully tactful and beautiful and tender, even for Adriance, who was tender with his valet and his stable-boy, with his old gondolier and the beggar-women who prayed to the saints for him.

The letter was from Granada, written in the Alhambra, as he sat by the fountain of the Patio di Lindaraxa. In the orange and box and citron trees about him the nightingales were singing all the unwritten and unwritable music in the world, and "*Je pense à mon amie,*" he wrote. The air was heavy with the warm fragrance of the South and full of the sound of splashing, running water, as it had been in a certain old garden in Florence, long ago. The sky was one great turquoise, heated until it glowed. The wonderful

Moorish arches threw graceful blue shadows all about him. He had sketched an outline of them on the margin of his note-paper. The subtleties of Arabic decoration had cast an unholy spell over him, and Christian art and the brutal exaggerations of Gothic architecture were no more for him. The soul of Théophile Gautier had entered into him, and Western civilization was a bad dream, easily forgotten. The Alhambra itself had from the first seemed perfectly familiar to him, and he knew that he must have trod that court, sleek and brown and obsequious, centuries before Ferdinand rode into Andalusia. The letter was full of confidences about his work, and delicate allusions to their old happy days of study and comradeship, and of her own work, still so warmly remembered and appreciatively discussed everywhere he went.

As Windermere folded the letter he felt that Adriance had divined the thing needed and had risen to it in his own wonderful way. The letter was consistently egotistical, and seemed to him even a trifle patronizing, yet it was just what she had wanted. He wondered whether all the gift-bearers, all the sons of genius, broke what they touched and blighted what they caressed thus. A strong realization of his brother's charm and intensity and power came over him; he felt the breath of that whirlwind of flame in which Adriance passed, consuming all in his path, and himself even more resolutely than he consumed others. Then he looked down at this white, burnt-out brand that lay before him. "Like him, isn't it?" she said, quietly, and Windermere felt in her voice the softness of the south wind in the spring.

"I think I can scarcely answer his letter, but when you see

him next you can do that for me. I want you to tell him many things from me, yet they can all be summed up in this: I want him to grow wholly into his best and greatest self, even at the cost of the dear boyishness that is half his charm to you and me. Do you understand me?"

"I know perfectly well what you mean," answered Windermere, thoughtfully. "I have often felt so about him myself. And yet it's difficult to prescribe for those creative fellows; so little makes, so little mars."

Katharine raised herself upon her elbow, and her face flushed with the feverish earnestness of her speech. "Ah, but it is the waste of himself that I mean; his lashing himself out on stupid and uncomprehending people until they take him at their own estimate. He can kindle marble, strike fire from putty, but is it worth what it costs him? Certainly there is a sacred and dignified selfishness which properly belongs to art and religion. You know how he wastes his time and strength in those idiotic social obligations which he takes so seriously—in chivalrous attentions to vapid old women who knew his mother, and in writing wedding-marches for every pink-and-white thing who asks him."

"Come, come," expostulated Windermere, alarmed at her excitement. "Where is the new sonata? Let him speak for himself."

He sat down at the piano and began playing the first movement of the sonata, which was indeed the voice of Adriance, his lofty and proper speech. The sonata was dedicated to Brahms, and was the most classic work Hilgarde had done up to that time. It marked, indeed, the transition from his purely lyric vein to that deeper and nobler style by which he will live. Windermere played intelligently, without the least affectation of virtuosity, but with that sympathetic comprehension which seems peculiar to a certain lovable class of men who never accomplish anything in particular. When he had finished he turned to Katharine.

"How he has grown! Heavens, how he has grown!" she cried. "This thing is entirely great. There is not a trace of that persistent saccharine quality that was always creeping into his earlier work. The theme, the whole conception is big and serene. How firm the texture is! and surely he never wrote such harmonies before. What the last three years have done for him! He used to write only the tragedies of passion; but this is the tragedy of the soul, the shadow co-existent with the soul. This is the tragedy of effort and failure, the thing Keats called hell. This is my tragedy, as I lie here spent by the white race course, listening to the feet of the runners as they pass me—ah, God! the swift feet of the runners!"

She turned her face away and covered it with her straining hands. Windermere crossed over to her quickly and knelt beside her. In all the days he had known her she had never before given voice to the bitterness of her own defeat beyond an occasional ironical jest. Her courage had become a point of pride with him, and to see it going sickened him.

"Don't do it," he gasped. "I can't stand it, I really can't, I feel it too much. We mustn't speak of that; it's too tragic and too vast."

When she turned her face back to him there was a ghost

of the old, brave, cynical smile on it, more bitter than the tears she could not shed. "No, I won't be so ungenerous; I will save that for the watches of the night when I have no better company. Now you may mix me another drink of some sort. Formerly, when it was not *if* I should ever sing Brunhilda, but quite simply when I *should* sing Brunhilda, I was always starving myself and thinking what I might drink and what I might not. But broken music-boxes may drink whatsoever they list, and no one cares whether they lose their figure. Run over that shepherd-boy theme at the beginning again. That, at least, is not new. It was running in his head when we were in Venice years ago, and he used to drum it on his glass at the dinner-table. He had just begun to work it out when the late autumn came on, and the paleness of the Adriatic oppressed him, and he decided to go to Florence for the winter, and lost touch with the theme during his illness. Do you remember those frightful days? All the people who have loved him are not strong enough to save him from himself! When I got word from Florence that he had been ill, I was in Nice filling a concert engagement. His wife was hurrying to him from Paris, but I reached him first. I arrived at dusk, in a terrific storm. They had taken an old palace there for the winter, and I found him in the library—a long, dark room full of old Latin books and heavy furniture and bronzes. He was sitting by a wood fire at one end of the room, looking, oh, so worn and pale!—as he always does when he is ill, you know. Ah, it is so good that you *do* know! Even his red smoking-jacket lent no color to his face. His first words were not to tell me how ill he had been, but that that morning he had been well enough to put the last strokes to the score of his '*Souvenirs d'Automne*,' and he was, as I most like to remember him, so calm and happy and tired; not gay, as he usually is, but just contented and tired with that heavenly tiredness that comes after a good work done at last. Outside, the rain poured down in torrents, and the wind moaned for the pain of all the world and sobbed in the branches of the shivering olives and about the walls of that desolated old palace. There was a concert piano in the room, and he played that prelude of Chopin's with the ceaseless pelting of rain-drops in the bass. He wrote it, you know, when George Sand carried him off to Majorca and shut him up in a damp grotto in the hill-side, and it rained forever and ever, and he had only goat's milk to drink. Adriance had been to Majorca, you know, and had slept in their grotto. How that night comes back to me! There were no lights in the room, only the wood fire which glowed upon the hard features of the bronze Dante like the reflection of purgatorial flames, and threw long black shadows about us; beyond us it scarcely penetrated the gloom at all. How heavy and impenetrable were those shadows! quite like the darkness of the under world, where it will be resting-time indeed, and the last strokes will have been put to the last score, and we shall all be together, resting in the common darkness, after it is all over. Suddenly Adriance stopped playing and sat staring at the fire with the weariness of all his life in his eyes, and of all the other lives that must aspire and suffer to make up one such life as his. Somehow the wind with all its world pain had got into the room, and the cold rain was in our eyes, and the wave came up in both of us at once—that awful vague, universal pain, that cold fear of life and death and God and hope—and we were like two clinging together on a spar in mid-ocean after the shipwreck of everything. Then we heard the front door open with a great gust of wind that shook even the walls, and the servants came running with lights, announcing that Madame had returned from Paris, '*and in the book we read no more that night.*' " She gave the old line with a certain bitter humor, and with the hard, bright smile in which of old she had wrapped her weakness as in a glittering garment. That ironical smile, worn like a mask through so many years, had gradually changed even the lines of her face completely, and when she looked in the mirror she saw not herself, but the scathing critic, the amused observer and satirist of herself. Sometimes while looking at the mask she wore, Windermere had thought of Richard's lines, "the shadow of my sorrow hath destroyed the shadow of my face." He dropped his head upon his hand and sat looking at the rug. "How much you have cared!" he said.

"Ah, yes, I cared," she said, closing her eyes with a long-drawn sigh of relief; and lying perfectly still, she went on: "You can't imagine what a comfort it is to have you know how I cared, what a relief it is to be able to tell it to someone. I used to want to shriek it out to the world in the long nights when I could not sleep. It seemed to me that I could not die with it. It demanded some sort of expression. And now that you know, you would scarcely believe how much less sharp the agony of it is."

Windermere continued to look helplessly at the floor. "I was not sure how much you wanted me to know," he said.

"Oh, I intended you should know from the first time I looked into your face, when you came that day with Charley. I flatter myself that I have been able to conceal it when I chose, though I suppose women always think that. The more observing ones may have seen, but discerning people are usually discreet and often kind, for we usually bleed a little before we begin to discern. But I wanted you to know; you are so like him that it is almost like telling him himself. At least, I feel now that he will know some day, and then I will be quite sacred from his compassion, for we none of us dare pity the dead. Since it was what my life has chiefly meant, I should like him to know. On the whole, I am not ashamed of it. I have fought a good fight."

"And has he never known at all?" asked Windermere, in a thick voice.

"Oh! never at all in the way that you mean. Of course he is accustomed to looking into the eyes of women and finding love there; when he doesn't find it there he thinks he must have been guilty of some discourtesy and is miserable about it. He has a genuine fondness for everyone who is not stupid or gloomy, or old or preternaturally ugly. Granted youth and cheerfulness, and a moderate amount of wit and some tact, and Adriance will always be glad to see you coming around the corner. I shared with the rest; shared the smiles and the gallantries and the droll little sermons. It was quite like a Sunday-school picnic; we wore our best clothes and a smile and took our turns. It was his kindness that was hardest. I have pretty well used my life up at standing punishment."

"Don't; you'll make me hate him," groaned Windermere.

Katharine laughed and began to play nervously with her fan. "It wasn't in the slightest degree his fault; that is the most grotesque part of it. Why, it had really begun before I ever met him. His early music was the first that ever really took hold of me. When I was a child out in Iowa, and Charley was braking on the road, I used to lie out under the apple-trees and dream about him. I had seen his picture in some magazine or other, and I always fancied him in Paris leading the gilded existence of a Ouida hero. I had a tough pull to get started; it was a long jump from Bird City to Chicago, and a longer one from Chicago to New York. I fought my way to him, and I drank my doom greedily enough."

Windermere rose and stood hesitating. "I think I must go. You ought to be quiet and I don't think I can hear any more just now."

She put out her hand and took his playfully. "You've put in three weeks at this sort of thing, haven't you? Well, it may never be to your glory in this world, perhaps, but it will stand to your credit in the land to which I travel. I wax quotational. It's been the mercy of heaven to me, and it ought to square accounts for a much worse life than yours will ever be. 'Unto one of the least of these,' you remember."

Windermere knelt beside her, saying, brokenly: "I stayed because I wanted to be with you, that's all. I have never cared about other women since I met you in New York when I was a lad. You are a part of my destiny, and I could not leave you if I would."

She put her hands on his shoulders and shook her head.

"No, no; don't tell me that. I have seen enough of the trag-edy of life, God knows: don't show me any more just as the curtain is going down. No, no, it was only a boy's fancy, and your divine pity and my utter pitiableness have recalled it for a moment. One does not love the dying, dear friend. If some fancy of that sort had been left over from boyhood, this would rid you of it, and that were well. Now go, and you will come again to-morrow, as long as there are tomor-rows, will you not?" She took his hand with a smile that lifted the mask from her soul, that was both courage and sadness, hope and despair, and full of infinite loyalty and tenderness, she said softly:

> *"For ever and for ever, farewell, Cassius;*
> *If we do meet again, why, we shall smile;*
> *If not, why then, this parting was well made."*

The courage in her eyes was like the clear light of a star to him as he went out.

On the night of Adriance Hilgarde's opening concert in Paris, Windermere sat by the bed in the ranch-house in Wyoming, watching over the last battle that we have with the flesh before we are done with it and free of it forever. At times it seemed that the serene soul of her must have left already and found some refuge from the storm, and only the tenacious animal life were left to do battle with death. She labored under a delusion at once pitiful and merciful, thinking that she was in the Pullman on her way to New York, going back to her life and her work. When she aroused from her stupor, it was only to ask the porter to waken her half an hour out of Jersey City, or to remonstrate with him about the roughness of the road, and to declare that she would never travel by that line again. At midnight Windermere and the nurse were left alone with her. Poor Charley Gaylord had lain down on a couch outside the door. Windermere sat looking at the sputtering night-lamp until it made his eyes ache. His head dropped forward on the foot of the bed and he sank into a heavy, distressful slumber. He was dreaming of Adriance's concert in Paris, and of Adriance, the troubadour, smiling and debonair, with his boyish face and the touch of silver gray in his hair. He heard the applause and he saw the roses going up over the footlights until they were stacked half as high as the piano, and the petals fell and scattered, making crimson splotches on the floor. Down this crimson pathway came Adriance with his youthful step, leading his prima donna by the hand; a dark woman this time, with Spanish eyes.

The nurse touched him on the shoulder, he started and awoke. She screened the lamp with her hand. Windermere saw that Katharine was awake and conscious, and struggling a little. He lifted her gently on his arm and began to fan her. She laid her hands lightly on his hair and looked into his face with eyes that seemed never to have wept or doubted. "Ah, dear Adriance, dear, dear," she whispered.

Windermere went to call her brother, but when they came back the madness of art was over for Katharine.

Two days later Windermere was pacing the station siding, waiting for the West-bound train. Charley Gaylord walked beside him, but the two men had nothing to say to each other. Windermere's bags were piled on the truck, and his step was hurried and his eyes were full of impatience, as he gazed again and again up the track, watching for the train. Gaylord's impatience was not less than his own; these two, who had grown so close, had now become painful and impossible to each other, and longed for the wrench of farewell.

As the train pulled in, Windermere wrung Gaylord's hand among the crowd of alighting passengers. The people of a German opera company, *en route* for the coast, rushed by them in frantic haste to snatch their breakfast during the stop. Windermere heard an exclamation in a broad South German dialect, and a massive woman whose figure persistently escaped from her stays in the most improbable places and whose florid face was marked by good living and champagne as by fine tide lines, rushed up to him, her blond hair disordered by the wind, and glowing with joyful surprise she caught his coat-sleeve with her tightly gloved hands.

"Herr Gott, Adriance, *lieber Freund,*" she cried, emotionally.

Windermere quickly withdrew his arm, and lifted his hat, blushing. "Pardon me, madame, but I see that you have mistaken me for Adriance Hilgarde. I am his brother," he said, quietly, and turning from the crestfallen singer he hurried into the car.

THE BOHEMIAN GIRL

THE TRANS-CONTINENTAL Express swung along the windings of the Sand River Valley, and in the rear seat of the observation car a young man sat greatly at his ease, not in the least discomfited by the fierce sunlight which beat in upon his brown face and neck and strong back. There was a look of relaxation and of great passivity about his broad shoulders, which seemed almost too heavy until he stood up and squared them. He wore a pale flannel shirt and a blue silk necktie with loose ends. His trousers were wide and belted at the waist, and his short sack-coat hung open. His heavy shoes had seen good service. His reddish-brown hair, like his clothes, had a foreign cut. He had deep-set, dark blue eyes under heavy reddish eyebrows. His face was kept clean only by close shaving, and even the sharpest razor left a glint of yellow in the smooth brown of his skin. His teeth and the palms of his hands were very white. His head, which looked hard and stubborn, lay indolently in the green cushion of the wicker chair, and as he looked out at the ripe summer country a teasing, not unkindly smile played over his lips. Once, as he basked thus comfortably, a quick light flashed in his eyes, curiously dilating the pupils, and his mouth became a hard, straight line, gradually relaxing into its former smile of rather kindly mockery. He told himself, apparently, that there was no point in getting excited; and he seemed a master hand at taking his ease when he could. Neither the sharp whistle of the locomotive nor the brakeman's call disturbed him. It was not until after the train had stopped that he rose, put on a Panama hat, took from the rack a small valise and a flute-case, and stepped deliberately to the station platform. The baggage was already unloaded, and the stranger presented a check for a battered sole-leather steamer-trunk.

"Can you keep it here for a day or two?" he asked the agent. "I may send for it, and I may not."

"Depends on whether you like the country, I suppose?" demanded the agent in a challenging tone.

"Just so."

The agent shrugged his shoulders, looked scornfully at the small trunk, which was marked "N.E.," and handed out a claim check without further comment. The stranger watched him as he caught one end of the trunk and dragged it into the express room. The agent's manner seemed to remind him of something amusing. "Doesn't seem to be a very big place," he remarked, looking about.

"It's big enough for us," snapped the agent, as he banged the trunk into a corner.

That remark, apparently, was what Nils Ericson had wanted. He chuckled quietly as he took a leather strap from his pocket and swung his valise around his shoulder. Then he settled his Panama securely on his head, turned up his trousers, tucked the flute-case under his arm, and started off across the fields. He gave the town, as he would have said, a wide berth, and cut through a great fenced pasture, emerging, when he rolled under the barbed wire at the farther corner, upon a white dusty road which ran straight up from the river valley to the high prairies, where the ripe wheat stood yellow and the tin roofs and weather-cocks were twinkling in the fierce sunlight. By the time Nils had done three miles, the sun was sinking and the farm-wagons on their way home from town came rattling by, covering him with dust and making him sneeze. When one of the farmers pulled up and offered to give him a lift, he clambered in willingly. The driver was a thin, grizzled old man with a long lean neck and a foolish sort of beard, like a goat's. "How fur ye goin'?" he asked, as he clucked to his horses and started off.

"Do you go by the Ericson place?"

"Which Ericson?" The old man drew in his reins as if he expected to stop again.

"Preacher Ericson's."

"Oh, the Old Lady Ericson's!" He turned and looked at Nils. "La, me! If you're goin' out there you might 'a' rid out in the automobile. That's a pity, now. The Old Lady Ericson was in town with her auto. You might 'a' heard it snortin' anywhere about the post-office er the butcher-shop."

"Has she a motor?" asked the stranger absently.

"'Deed an' she has! She runs into town every night about this time for her mail and meat for supper. Some folks say she's afraid her auto won't get exercise enough, but I say that's jealousy."

"Aren't there any other motors about here?"

"Oh, yes! we have fourteen in all. But nobody else gets around like the Old Lady Ericson. She's out, rain er shine, over the whole county, chargin' into town and out amongst her farms, an' up to her sons' places. Sure you ain't goin' to the wrong place?" He craned his neck and looked at Nils' flute case with eager curiosity. "The old woman ain't got any piany that I knows on. Olaf, he has a grand. His wife's musical; took lessons in Chicago."

"I'm going up there tomorrow," said Nils imperturbably. He saw that the driver took him for a piano-tuner.

"Oh, I see!" The old man screwed up his eyes mysteriously. He was a little dashed by the stranger's non-communicativeness, but he soon broke out again.

"I'm one o' Mis' Ericson's tenants. Look after one of her places. I did own the place myself oncet, but I lost it a while back, in the bad years just after the World's Fair. Just as well, too, I say. Lets you out o' payin' taxes. The Ericsons do own most of the county now. I remember the old preacher's fav'rite text used to be, 'To them that hath shall be given.' They've spread something wonderful—run over this here country like bindweed. But I ain't one that begretches it to 'em. Folks is entitled to what they kin git; and they're hustlers. Olaf, he's in the Legislature now, and a likely man fur Congress. Listen, if that ain't the old woman comin' now. Want I should stop her?"

Nils shook his head. He heard the deep chug-chug of a motor vibrating steadily in the clear twilight behind them. The pale lights of the car swam over the hill, and the old man slapped his reins and turned clear out of the road, ducking his head at the first of three angry snorts from behind. The motor was running at a hot, even speed, and passed without turning an inch from its course. The driver was a stalwart woman who sat at ease in the front seat and drove her car bare-headed. She left a cloud of dust and a trail of gasoline behind her. Her tenant threw back his head and sneezed.

"Whew! I sometimes say I'd as lief be *before* Mrs. Ericson as behind her. She does beat all! Nearly seventy, and never lets another soul touch that car. Puts it into commission herself every morning, and keeps it tuned up by the hitch-bar all day. I never stop work for a drink o' water that I don't hear her a-churnin' up the road. I reckon her darter-in-laws never sets down easy nowadays. Never know when she'll pop in. Mis' Otto, she says to me: 'We're so afraid that thing'll blow up and do Ma some injury yet, she's so turrible venturesome.' Says I: 'I wouldn't stew, Mis' Otto; the old lady'll drive that car to the funeral of every darter-in-law she's got.' That was after the old woman had jumped a turrible bad culvert."

The stranger heard vaguely what the old man was saying. Just now he was experiencing something very much like homesickness, and he was wondering what had brought it about. The mention of a name or two, perhaps; the rattle of a wagon along a dusty road; the rank, resinous smell of sunflowers and ironweed, which the night damp brought up from the draws and low places; perhaps, more than all, the dancing lights of the motor that had plunged by. He squared his shoulders with a comfortable sense of strength.

The wagon, as it jolted westward, climbed a pretty steady upgrade. The country, receding from the rough river valley, swelled more and more gently, as if it had been smoothed out by the wind. On one of the last of the rugged ridges, at the end of a branch road, stood a grim square house with a tin roof and double porches. Behind the house stretched a row of broken, wind-racked poplars, and down the hill slope to the left straggled the sheds and stables. The old man stopped his horses where the Ericsons' road branched across a dry sand creek that wound about the foot of the hill.

"That's the old lady's place. Want I should drive in?"

"No, thank you. I'll roll out here. Much obliged to you. Good night."

His passenger stepped down over the front wheel, and the old man drove on reluctantly, looking back as if he would like to see how the stranger would be received.

As Nils was crossing the dry creek he heard the restive tramp of a horse coming toward him down the hill. Instantly he flashed out of the road and stood behind a thicket of wild plum bushes that grew in the sandy bed. Peering through the dusk, he saw a light horse, under tight rein, descending the hill at a sharp walk. The rider was a slender woman—barely visible against the dark hillside—wearing an old-fashioned derby hat and a long riding skirt. She sat lightly in the saddle, with her chin high, and seemed to be looking into the distance. As she passed the plum thicket her horse snuffed the air and shied. She struck him, pulling him in sharply, with an angry exclamation, "*Blázne!*" in Bohemian. Once in the main road, she let him out into a lope, and they soon emerged upon the crest of high land, where they moved along the skyline, silhouetted against the band of faint color that lingered in the west. This horse and rider, with their free, rhythmical gallop, were the only moving things to be seen on the face of the flat country. They seemed, in the last sad light of evening, not to be there accidentally, but as an inevitable detail of the landscape.

Nils watched them until they had shrunk to a mere moving speck against the sky, then he crossed the sand creek and climbed the hill. When he reached the gate the front of the house was dark, but a light was shining from the side windows. The pigs were squealing in the hog corral, and Nils could see a tall boy, who carried two big wooden buckets, moving about among them. Half way between the barn and the house, the windmill wheezed lazily. Following the path that ran around to the back porch, Nils stopped to look through the screen door into the lamp-lit kitchen. The kitchen was the largest room in the house; Nils remembered that his older brothers used to give dances there when he was a boy. Beside the stove stood a little girl with two light yellow braids and a broad, flushed face, peering anxiously into a frying-pan. In the dining-room beyond, a large, broad-shouldered woman was moving about the table. She walked with an active, springy step. Her face was heavy and florid, almost without wrinkles, and her hair was black at seventy. Nils felt proud of her as he watched her deliberate activity; never a momentary hesitation, or a movement that did not tell. He waited until she came out into the kitchen and, brushing the child aside, took her place at the stove. Then he tapped on the screen door and entered.

"It's nobody but Nils, Mother. I expect you weren't looking for me."

Mrs. Ericson turned away from the stove and stood staring at him. "Bring the lamp, Hilda, and let me look."

Nils laughed and unslung his valise. "What's the matter, Mother? Don't you know me?"

Mrs. Ericson put down the lamp. "You must be Nils. You don't look very different, anyway."

"Nor you, Mother. You hold your own. Don't you wear glasses yet?"

"Only to read by. Where's your trunk, Nils?"

"Oh, I left that in town. I thought it might not be convenient for you to have company so near threshing-time."

"Don't be foolish, Nils." Mrs. Ericson turned back to the stove. "I don't thresh now. I hitched the wheat land onto the next farm and have a tenant. Hilda, take some hot water up to the company room, and go call little Eric."

The tow-haired child, who had been standing in mute amazement, took up the tea-kettle and withdrew, giving Nils a long, admiring look from the door of the kitchen stairs.

"Who's the youngster?" Nils asked, dropping down on the bench behind the kitchen stove.

"One of your Cousin Henrik's."

"How long has Cousin Henrik been dead?"

"Six years. There are two boys. One stays with Peter and one with Anders. Olaf is their guardeen."

There was a clatter of pails on the porch, and a tall, lanky boy peered wonderingly in through the screen door. He had a fair, gentle face and big gray eyes, and wisps of soft yellow hair hung down under his cap. Nils sprang up and pulled him into the kitchen, hugging him and slapping him on the shoulders. "Well, if it isn't my kid! Look at the size of him! Don't you know me, Eric?"

The boy reddened under his sunburn and freckles, and hung his head. "I guess it's Nils," he said shyly.

"You're a good guesser," laughed Nils, giving the lad's hand a swing. To himself he was thinking: "That's why the little girl looked so friendly. He's taught her to like me. He was only six when I went away, and he's remembered for twelve years."

Eric stood fumbling with his cap and smiling. "You look just like I thought you would," he ventured.

"Go wash your hands, Eric," called Mrs. Ericson. "I've got cob corn for supper, Nils. You used to like it. I guess you don't get much of that in the old country. Here's Hilda; she'll take you up to your room. You'll want to get the dust off you before you eat."

Mrs. Ericson went into the dining-room to lay another plate, and the little girl came up and nodded to Nils as if to let him know that his room was ready. He put out his hand and she took it, with a startled glance up at his face. Little Eric dropped his towel, threw an arm about Nils and one about Hilda, gave them a clumsy squeeze, and then stumbled out to the porch.

During supper Nils heard exactly how much land each of his eight grown brothers farmed, how their crops were coming on, and how much live stock they were feeding. His mother watched him narrowly as she talked. "You've got better looking, Nils," she remarked abruptly, whereupon he grinned and the children giggled. Eric, although he was eighteen and as tall as Nils, was always accounted a child, being the last of so many sons. His face seemed child-like, too, Nils thought, and he had the open, wandering eyes of a little boy. All the others had been men at his age.

After supper Nils went out to the front porch and sat down on the step to smoke a pipe. Mrs. Ericson drew a rocking-chair up near him and began to knit busily. It was one of the few old-world customs she had kept up, for she could not bear to sit with idle hands.

"Where's little Eric, Mother?"

"He's helping Hilda with the dishes. He does it of his own will; I don't like a boy to be too handy about the house."

"He seems like a nice kid."

"He's very obedient."

Nils smiled a little in the dark. It was just as well to shift the line of conversation. "What are you knitting there, Mother?"

"Baby stockings. The boys keep me busy." Mrs. Ericson chuckled and clicked her needles.

"How many grandchildren have you?"

"Only thirty-one now. Olaf lost his three. They were sickly, like their mother."

"I supposed he had a second crop by this time!"

"His second wife has no children. She's too proud. She tears about on horseback all the time. But she'll get caught up with, yet. She sets herself very high, though nobody knows what for. They were low enough Bohemians she came of. I never thought much of Bohemians; always drinking."

Nils puffed away at his pipe in silence, and Mrs. Ericson knitted on. In a few moments she added grimly: "She was down here to-night, just before you came. She'd like to quarrel with me and come between me and Olaf, but I don't give her the chance. I suppose you'll be bringing a wife home some day."

"I don't know. I've never thought much about it."

"Well, perhaps it's best as it is," suggested Mrs. Ericson hopefully. "You'd never be contented tied down to the land. There was roving blood in your father's family, and it's come out in you. I expect your own way of life suits you best." Mrs. Ericson had dropped into a blandly agreeable tone which Nils well remembered. It seemed to amuse him a good deal and his white teeth flashed behind his pipe. His mother's strategies had always diverted him, even when he was a boy—they were so flimsy and patent, so illy proportioned to her vigor and force. "They've been waiting to see which way I'd jump," he reflected. He felt that Mrs. Ericson was pondering his case deeply as she sat clicking her needles.

"I don't suppose you've ever got used to steady work," she went on presently. "Men ain't apt to if they roam around too long. It's a pity you didn't come back the year after the World's Fair. Your father picked up a good bit of land cheap then, in the hard times, and I expect maybe he'd have give you a farm. It's too bad you put off comin' back so long, for I always thought he meant to do something by you."

Nils laughed and shook the ashes out of his pipe. "I'd have missed a lot if I had come back then. But I'm sorry I didn't get back to see father."

"Well, I suppose we have to miss things at one end or the other. Perhaps you are as well satisfied with your own doings, now, as you'd have been with a farm," said Mrs. Ericson reassuringly.

"Land's a good thing to have," Nils commented, as he lit another match and sheltered it with his hand.

His mother looked sharply at his face until the match burned out. "Only when you stay on it!" she hastened to say.

Eric came round the house by the path just then, and Nils rose, with a yawn. "Mother, if you don't mind, Eric and I will take a little tramp before bed-time. It will make me sleep."

"Very well; only don't stay long. I'll sit up and wait for you. I like to lock up myself."

Nils put his hand on Eric's shoulder, and the two tramped down the hill and across the sand creek into the dusty high-road beyond. Neither spoke. They swung along at an even gait, Nils puffing at his pipe. There was no moon, and the white road and the wide fields lay faint in the starlight. Over everything was darkness and thick silence, and the smell of dust and sunflowers. The brothers followed the road for a mile or more without finding a place to sit down. Finally, Nils perched on a stile over the wire fence, and Eric sat on the lower step.

"I began to think you never would come back, Nils," said the boy softly.

"Didn't I promise you I would?"

"Yes; but people don't bother about promises they make to babies. Did you really know you were going away for good when you went to Chicago with the cattle that time?"

"I thought it very likely, if I could make my way."

"I don't see how you did it, Nils. Not many fellows could." Eric rubbed his shoulder against his brother's knee.

"The hard thing was leaving home—you and father. It was easy enough, once I got beyond Chicago. Of course I got awful homesick; used to cry myself to sleep. But I'd burned my bridges."

"You had always wanted to go, hadn't you?"

"Always. Do you still sleep in our little room? Is that cottonwood still by the window?"

Eric nodded eagerly and smiled up at his brother in the gray darkness.

"You remember how we always said the leaves were whispering when they rustled at night? Well, they always whispered to me about the sea. Sometimes they said names out of the geography books. In a high wind they had a desperate sound, like something trying to tear loose."

"How funny, Nils," said Eric dreamily, resting his chin on his hand. "That tree still talks like that, and 'most always it talks to me about you."

They sat a while longer, watching the stars. At last Eric whispered anxiously: "Hadn't we better go back now? Mother will get tired waiting for us." They rose and took a short cut home, through the pasture.

II

The next morning Nils woke with the first flood of light that came with dawn. The white-plastered walls of his room reflected the glare that shone through the thin window-shades, and he found it impossible to sleep. He dressed hurriedly and slipped down the hall and up the back stairs to the half-story room which he used to share with his little brother. Eric, in a skimpy night-shirt, was sitting on the edge of the bed, rubbing his eyes, his pale yellow hair standing up in tufts all over his head. When he saw Nils, he murmured something confusedly and hustled his long legs into his trousers. "I didn't expect you'd be up so early, Nils," he said, as his head emerged from his blue shirt.

"Oh, you thought I was a dude, did you?" Nils gave him a playful tap which bent the tall boy up like a clasp-knife. "See here; I must teach you to box." Nils thrust his hands into his pockets and walked about. "You haven't changed things much up here. Got most of my old traps, haven't you?"

He took down a bent, withered piece of sapling that hung over the dresser. "If this isn't the stick Lou Sandberg killed himself with!"

The boy looked up from his shoe-lacing.

"Yes; you never used to let me play with that. Just how did he do it, Nils? You were with father when he found Lou, weren't you?"

"Yes. Father was going off to preach somewhere, and, as we drove along, Lou's place looked sort of forlorn, and we thought we'd stop and cheer him up. When we found him father said he'd been dead a couple days. He'd tied a piece of binding twine round his neck, made a noose in each end, fixed the nooses over the ends of a bent stick, and let the stick spring straight; strangled himself."

"What made him kill himself such a silly way?"

The simplicity of the boy's question set Nils laughing. He clapped little Eric on the shoulder. "What made him such a silly as to kill himself at all, I should say!"

"Oh, well! But his hogs had the cholera, and all up and died on him, didn't they?"

"Sure they did; but he didn't have cholera; and there were plenty of hogs left in the world, weren't there?"

"Well, but, if they weren't his, how could they do him any good?" Eric asked, in astonishment.

"Oh, scat! He could have had lots of fun with other people's hogs. He was a chump, Lou Sandberg. To kill yourself for a pig—think of that, now!" Nils laughed all the way downstairs, and quite embarrassed little Eric, who fell to scrubbing his face and hands at the tin basin. While he was parting his wet hair at the kitchen looking-glass, a heavy tread sounded on the stairs. The boy dropped his comb. "Gracious, there's Mother. We must have talked too long." He hurried out to the shed, slipped on his overalls, and disappeared with the milking pails.

Mrs. Ericson came in, wearing a clean white apron, her black hair shining from the application of a wet brush.

"Good morning, Mother. Can't I make the fire for you?"

"No, thank you, Nils. It's no trouble to make a cob fire, and I like to manage the kitchen stove myself." Mrs. Ericson paused with a shovel full of ashes in her hand. "I expect you will be wanting to see your brothers as soon as possible. I'll take you up to Anders' place this morning. He's threshing, and most of our boys are over there."

"Will Olaf be there?"

Mrs. Ericson went on taking out the ashes, and spoke

between shovels. "No; Olaf's wheat is all in, put away in his new barn. He got six thousand bushel this year. He's going to town to-day to get men to finish roofing his barn."

"So Olaf is building a new barn?" Nils asked absently.

"Biggest one in the county, and almost done. You'll likely be here for the barn-raising. He's going to have a supper and a dance as soon as everybody's done threshing. Says it keeps the voters in a good humor. I tell him that's all non-sense; but Olaf has a long head for politics."

"Does Olaf farm all Cousin Henrik's land?"

Mrs. Ericson frowned as she blew into the faint smoke curling up about the cobs. "Yes; he holds it in trust for the children, Hilda and her brothers. He keeps strict account of everything he raises on it, and puts the proceeds out at compound interest for them."

Nils smiled as he watched the little flames shoot up. The door of the back stairs opened, and Hilda emerged, her arms behind her, buttoning up her long gingham apron as she came. He nodded to her gaily, and she twinkled at him out of her little blue eyes, set far apart over her wide cheek-bones.

"There, Hilda, you grind the coffee—and just put in an extra handful; I expect your Cousin Nils likes his strong," said Mrs. Ericson, as she went out to the shed.

Nils turned to look at the little girl, who gripped the cof-fee-grinder between her knees and ground so hard that her two braids bobbed and her face flushed under its broad spattering of freckles. He noticed on her middle finger something that had not been there last night, and that had evidently been put on for company: a tiny gold ring with a clumsily set garnet stone. As her hand went round and round he touched the ring with the tip of his finger, smiling.

Hilda glanced toward the shed door through which Mrs. Ericson had disappeared. "My Cousin Clara gave me that," she whispered bashfully. "She's Cousin Olaf's wife."

III

———

Mrs. Olaf Ericson—Clara Vavrika, as many people still called her—was moving restlessly about her big bare house that morning. Her husband had left for the county town before his wife was out of bed—her lateness in rising was one of the many things the Ericson family had against her. Clara seldom came downstairs before eight o'clock, and this morning she was even later, for she had dressed with unusual care. She put on, however, only a tight-fitting black dress, which people thereabouts thought very plain. She was a tall, dark woman of thirty, with a rather sallow complexion and a touch of dull salmon red in her cheeks, where the blood seemed to burn under her brown skin. Her hair, parted evenly above her low forehead, was so black that there were distinctly blue lights in it. Her black eyebrows were delicate half-moons and her lashes were long and heavy. Her eyes slanted a little, as if she had a strain of Tartar or gypsy blood, and were sometimes full of fiery determination and sometimes dull and opaque. Her expression was never altogether amiable; was often, indeed, distinctly sullen, or, when she was animated, sarcastic. She was most attractive in profile, for then one saw to advantage her small, well-shaped head and delicate ears, and felt at once that here was a very positive, if not an altogether pleasing, personality.

The entire management of Mrs. Olaf's household devolved upon her aunt, Johanna Vavrika, a superstitious, doting woman of fifty. When Clara was a little girl her mother died, and Johanna's life had been spent in ungrudging service to her niece. Clara, like many self-willed and discontented persons, was really very apt, without knowing it, to do as other people told her, and to let her destiny be decided for her by intelligences much below her own. It was her Aunt Johanna who had humored and spoiled her in her girlhood, who had got her off to Chicago to study piano, and who had finally persuaded her to marry Olaf Ericson as the best match she would be likely to make in that part of the country. Johanna Vavrika had been deeply scarred by smallpox in the old country. She was short and fat, homely and jolly and sentimental. She was so broad, and took such short steps when she walked, that her brother, Joe Vavrika, always called her his duck. She adored her niece because of her talent, because of her good looks and masterful ways, but most of all because of her selfishness.

Clara's marriage with Olaf Ericson was Johanna's particular triumph. She was inordinately proud of Olaf's position, and she found a sufficiently exciting career in managing Clara's house, in keeping it above the criticism of the Ericsons, in pampering Olaf to keep him from finding fault with his wife, and in concealing from every one Clara's domestic infelicities. While Clara slept of a morning, Johanna Vavrika was bustling about, seeing that Olaf and the men had their breakfast, and that the cleaning or the butter-making or the washing was properly begun by the two girls in the kitchen. Then, at about eight o'clock, she would take Clara's coffee up to her, and chat with her while she drank it, telling her what was going on in the house. Old Mrs. Ericson frequently said that her daughter-in-law would not know what day of the week it was if Johanna did not tell her every morning. Mrs. Ericson despised and pitied Johanna, but did not wholly dislike her. The one thing she hated in her daughter-in-law above everything else was the way in which Clara could come it over people. It enraged her that the affairs of her son's big, barnlike house went on as well as they did, and she used to feel that in this world we have to wait over-long to see the guilty punished. "Suppose Johanna Vavrika died or got sick?" the old lady used to say to Olaf. "Your wife wouldn't know where to look for her own dish-cloth." Olaf only shrugged his shoulders. The fact remained that Johanna did not die, and, although Mrs. Ericson often told her she was looking poorly, she was never ill. She seldom left the house, and she slept in a little room off the kitchen. No Ericson, by night or day, could come prying about there to find fault without her knowing it. Her one weakness was that she was an incurable talker, and she sometimes made trouble without meaning to.

This morning Clara was tying a wine-colored ribbon about her throat when Johanna appeared with her coffee. After putting the tray on a sewing-table, she began to make Clara's bed, chattering the while in Bohemian.

"Well, Olaf got off early, and the girls are baking. I'm

going down presently to make some poppy-seed bread for Olaf. He asked for prune preserves at breakfast, and I told him I was out of them, and to bring some prunes and honey and cloves from town."

Clara poured her coffee. "Ugh! I don't see how men can eat so much sweet stuff. In the morning, too!"

Her aunt chuckled knowingly. "Bait a bear with honey, as we say in the old country."

"Was he cross?" her niece asked indifferently.

"Olaf? Oh, no! He was in fine spirits. He's never cross if you know how to take him. I never knew a man to make so little fuss about bills. I gave him a list of things to get a yard long, and he didn't say a word; just folded it up and put it in his pocket."

"I can well believe he didn't say a word," Clara remarked with a shrug. "Some day he'll forget how to talk."

"Oh, but they say he's a grand speaker in the Legislature. He knows when to keep quiet. That's why he's got such influence in politics. The people have confidence in him." Johanna beat up a pillow and held it under her fat chin while she slipped on the case. Her niece laughed.

"Maybe we could make people believe we were wise, Aunty, if we held our tongues. Why did you tell Mrs. Ericson that Norman threw me again last Saturday and turned my foot? She's been talking to Olaf."

Johanna fell into great confusion. "Oh, but, my precious, the old lady asked for you, and she's always so angry if I can't give an excuse. Anyhow, she needn't talk; she's always tearing up something with that motor of hers."

When her aunt clattered down to the kitchen, Clara

went to dust the parlor. Since there was not much there to dust, this did not take very long. Olaf had built the house new for her before their marriage, but her interest in furnishing it had been short-lived. It went, indeed, little beyond a bath-tub and her piano. They had disagreed about almost every other article of furniture, and Clara had said she would rather have her house empty than full of things she didn't want. The house was set in a hillside, and the west windows of the parlor looked out above the kitchen yard thirty feet below. The east windows opened directly into the front yard. At one of the latter, Clara, while she was dusting, heard a low whistle. She did not turn at once, but listened intently as she drew her cloth slowly along the round of a chair. Yes, there it was:

"I dreamt that I dwelt in ma-a-arble halls."

She turned and saw Nils Ericson laughing in the sunlight, his hat in his hand, just outside the window. As she crossed the room he leaned against the wire screen. "Aren't you at all surprised to see me, Clara Vavrika?"

"No; I was expecting to see you. Mother Ericson telephoned Olaf last night that you were here."

Nils squinted and gave a long whistle. "Telephoned? That must have been while Eric and I were out walking. Isn't she enterprising? Lift this screen, won't you?"

Clara lifted the screen, and Nils swung his leg across the window-sill. As he stepped into the room she said: "You didn't think you were going to get ahead of your mother, did you?"

He threw his hat on the piano. "Oh, I do sometimes. You see, I'm ahead of her now. I'm supposed to be in Anders' wheat-field. But, as we were leaving, Mother ran her car into a soft place beside the road and sank up to the hubs. While they were going for horses to pull her out, I cut away behind the stacks and escaped." Nils chuckled. Clara's dull eyes lit up as she looked at him admiringly.

"You've got them guessing already. I don't know what your mother said to Olaf over the telephone, but he came back looking as if he'd seen a ghost, and he didn't go to bed until a dreadful hour—ten o'clock, I should think. He sat out on the porch in the dark like a graven image. It had been one of his talkative days, too." They both laughed, easily and lightly, like people who have laughed a great deal together; but they remained standing.

"Anders and Otto and Peter looked as if they had seen ghosts, too, over in the threshing-field. What's the matter with them all?"

Clara gave him a quick, searching look. "Well, for one thing, they've always been afraid you have the other will."

Nils looked interested. "The other will?"

"Yes. A later one. They knew your father made another, but they never knew what he did with it. They almost tore the old house to pieces looking for it. They always suspected that he carried on a clandestine correspondence with you, for the one thing he would do was to get his own mail himself. So they thought he might have sent the new will to you for safe-keeping. The old one, leaving everything to your mother, was made long before you went away, and it's understood among them that it cuts you out—that she will leave all the property to the others. Your father made the second will to prevent that. I've been hoping you had it. It would be such fun to spring it on them." Clara laughed mirthfully, a thing she did not often do now.

Nils shook his head reprovingly. "Come, now, you're malicious."

"No, I'm not. But I'd like something to happen to stir them all up, just for once. There never was such a family for having nothing ever happen to them but dinner and threshing. I'd almost be willing to die, just to have a funeral. *You* wouldn't stand it for three weeks."

Nils bent over the piano and began pecking at the keys with the finger of one hand. "I wouldn't? My dear young lady, how do you know what I can stand? *You* wouldn't wait to find out."

Clara flushed darkly and frowned. "I didn't believe you would ever come back—" she said defiantly.

"Eric believed I would, and he was only a baby when I went away. However, all's well that ends well, and I haven't come back to be a skeleton at the feast. We mustn't quarrel. Mother will be here with a search-warrant pretty soon." He swung round and faced her, thrusting his hands into his coat pockets. "Come, you ought to be glad to see me, if you want something to happen. I'm something, even without a will. We can have a little fun, can't we? I think we can!"

She echoed him, "I think we can!" They both laughed and their eyes sparkled. Clara Vavrika looked ten years younger than when she had put the velvet ribbon about her throat that morning.

"You know, I'm so tickled to see mother," Nils went on.

"I didn't know I was so proud of her. A regular pile-driver. How about little pigtails, down at the house? Is Olaf doing the square thing by those children?"

Clara frowned pensively. "Olaf has to do something that looks like the square thing, now that he's a public man!" She glanced drolly at Nils. "But he makes a good commission out of it. On Sundays they all get together here and figure. He lets Peter and Anders put in big bills for the keep of the two boys, and he pays them out of the estate. They are always having what they call accountings. Olaf gets something out of it, too. I don't know just how they do it, but it's entirely a family matter, as they say. And when the Ericsons say that—" Clara lifted her eyebrows.

Just then the angry *honk-honk* of an approaching motor sounded from down the road. Their eyes met and they began to laugh. They laughed as children do when they can not contain themselves, and can not explain the cause of their mirth to grown people, but share it perfectly together. When Clara Vavrika sat down at the piano after he was gone, she felt that she had laughed away a dozen years. She practised as if the house were burning over her head.

When Nils greeted his mother and climbed into the front seat of the motor beside her, Mrs. Ericson looked grim, but she made no comment upon his truancy until she had turned her car and was retracing her revolutions along the road that ran by Olaf's big pasture. Then she remarked dryly:

"If I were you I wouldn't see too much of Olaf's wife while you are here. She's the kind of woman who can't see much of men without getting herself talked about. She was a good deal talked about before he married her."

"Hasn't Olaf tamed her?" Nils asked indifferently.

Mrs. Ericson shrugged her massive shoulders. "Olaf don't seem to have much luck, when it comes to wives. The first one was meek enough, but she was always ailing. And this one has her own way. He says if he quarreled with her she'd go back to her father, and then he'd lose the Bohemian vote. There are a great many Bohunks in this district. But when you find a man under his wife's thumb you can always be sure there's a soft spot in him somewhere."

Nils thought of his own father, and smiled. "She brought him a good deal of money, didn't she, besides the Bohemian vote?"

Mrs. Ericson sniffed. "Well, she has a fair half section in her own name, but I can't see as that does Olaf much good. She will have a good deal of property some day, if old Vavrika don't marry again. But I don't consider a saloonkeeper's money as good as other people's money."

Nils laughed outright. "Come, Mother, don't let your prejudices carry you that far. Money's money. Old Vavrika's a mighty decent sort of saloonkeeper. Nothing rowdy about him."

Mrs. Ericson spoke up angrily: "Oh, I know you always stood up for them! But hanging around there when you were a boy never did you any good, Nils, nor any of the other boys who went there. There weren't so many after her when she married Olaf, let me tell you. She knew enough to grab her chance."

Nils settled back in his seat. "Of course I liked to go there, Mother, and you were always cross about it. You never took the trouble to find out that it was the one jolly house in this country for a boy to go to. All the rest of you were working yourselves to death, and the houses were mostly a mess, full of babies and washing and flies. Oh, it was all right—I understand that; but you are young only once, and I happened to be young then. Now, Vavrika's was always jolly. He played the violin, and I used to take my flute, and Clara played the piano, and Johanna used to sing Bohemian songs. She always had a big supper for us—herrings and pickles and poppy-seed bread, and lots of cake and preserves. Old Joe had been in the army in the old country, and he could tell lots of good stories. I can see him cutting bread, at the head of the table, now. I don't know what I'd have done when I was a kid if it hadn't been for the Vavrikas, really."

"And all the time he was taking money that other people had worked hard in the fields for," Mrs. Ericson observed.

"So do the circuses, Mother, and they're a good thing. People ought to get fun for some of their money. Even father liked old Joe."

"Your father," Mrs. Ericson said grimly, "liked everybody."

As they crossed the sand creek and turned into her own place, Mrs. Ericson observed, "There's Olaf's buggy. He's stopped on his way from town." Nils shook himself and prepared to greet his brother, who was waiting on the porch.

Olaf was a big, heavy Norwegian, slow of speech and

movement. His head was large and square, like a block of wood. When Nils, at a distance, tried to remember what his brother looked like, he could recall only his heavy head, high forehead, large nostrils, and pale blue eyes, set far apart. Olaf's features were rudimentary: the thing one noticed was the face itself, wide and flat and pale, devoid of any expression, betraying his fifty years as little as it betrayed anything else, and powerful by reason of its very stolidness. When Olaf shook hands with Nils he looked at him from under his light eyebrows, but Nils felt that no one could ever say what that pale look might mean. The one thing he had always felt in Olaf was a heavy stubbornness, like the unyielding stickiness of wet loam against the plow. He had always found Olaf the most difficult of his brothers.

"How do you do, Nils? Expect to stay with us long?"

"Oh, I may stay forever," Nils answered gaily. "I like this country better than I used to."

"There's been some work put into it since you left," Olaf remarked.

"Exactly. I think it's about ready to live in now—and I'm about ready to settle down." Nils saw his brother lower his big head. ("Exactly like a bull," he thought.) "Mother's been persuading me to slow down now, and go in for farming," he went on lightly.

Olaf made a deep sound in his throat. "Farming ain't learned in a day," he brought out, still looking at the ground.

"Oh, I know! But I pick things up quickly." Nils had not meant to antagonize his brother, and he did not know now why he was doing it. "Of course," he went on, "I shouldn't expect to make a big success, as you fellows have done. But then, I'm not ambitious. I won't want much. A little land, and some cattle, maybe."

Olaf still stared at the ground, his head down. He wanted to ask Nils what he had been doing all these years, that he didn't have a business somewhere he couldn't afford to leave; why he hadn't more pride than to come back with only a little sole-leather trunk to show for himself, and to present himself as the only failure in the family. He did not ask one of these questions, but he made them all felt distinctly.

"Humph!" Nils thought. "No wonder the man never talks, when he can butt his ideas into you like that without ever saying a word. I suppose he uses that kind of smokeless powder on his wife all the time. But I guess she has her innings." He chuckled, and Olaf looked up. "Never mind me, Olaf. I laugh without knowing why, like little Eric. He's another cheerful dog."

"Eric," said Olaf slowly, "is a spoiled kid. He's just let his mother's best cow go dry because he don't milk her right. I was hoping you'd take him away somewhere and put him into business. If he don't do any good among strangers, he never will." This was a long speech for Olaf, and as he finished it he climbed into his buggy.

Nils shrugged his shoulders. "Same old tricks," he thought. "Hits from behind you every time. What a whale of a man!" He turned and went round to the kitchen, where his mother was scolding little Eric for letting the gasoline get low.

IV

Joe Vavrika's saloon was not in the county-seat, where Olaf and Mrs. Ericson did their trading, but in a cheerfuller place, a little Bohemian settlement which lay at the other end of the county, ten level miles north of Olaf's farm. Clara rode up to see her father almost every day. Vavrika's house was, so to speak, in the back yard of his saloon. The garden between the two buildings was inclosed by a high board fence as tight as a partition, and in summer Joe kept beer tables and wooden benches among the gooseberry bushes under his little cherry tree. At one of these tables Nils Ericson was seated in the late afternoon, three days after his return home. Joe had gone in to serve a customer, and Nils was lounging on his elbows, looking rather mournfully into his half-emptied pitcher, when he heard a laugh across the little garden. Clara, in her riding-habit, was standing at the back door of the house, under the grapevine trellis that old Joe had grown there long ago. Nils rose.

"Come out and keep your father and me company. We've been gossiping all afternoon. Nobody to bother us but the flies."

She shook her head. "No, I never come out here any more. Olaf doesn't like it. I must live up to my position, you know."

"You mean to tell me you never come out and chat with the boys, as you used to? He *has* tamed you! Who keeps up these flower-beds?"

"I come out on Sundays, when father is alone, and read

the Bohemian papers to him. But I am never here when the bar is open. What have you two been doing?"

"Talking, as I told you. I've been telling him about my travels. I find I can't talk much at home, not even to Eric."

Clara reached up and poked with her riding-whip at a white moth that was fluttering in the sunlight among the vine leaves. "I suppose you will never tell me about all those things."

"Where can I tell them? Not in Olaf's house, certainly. What's the matter with our talking here?" He pointed persuasively with his hat to the bushes and the green table, where the flies were singing lazily above the empty beer-glasses.

Clara shook her head weakly. "No, it wouldn't do. Besides, I am going now."

"I'm on Eric's mare. Would you be angry if I overtook you?"

Clara looked back and laughed. "You might try and see. I can leave you if I don't want you. Eric's mare can't keep up with Norman."

Nils went into the bar and attempted to pay his score. Big Joe, six feet four, with curly yellow hair and mustache, clapped him on the shoulder. "Not a God-damn a your money go in my drawer, you hear? Only next time you bring your flute, te-te-te-te-te-ty." Joe wagged his fingers in imitation of the flute player's position. "My Clara, she come all-a-time Sundays an' play for me. She not like to play at Ericson's place." He shook his yellow curls and laughed. "Not a God-damn a fun at Ericson's. You come a Sunday. You like-a fun. No forget de flute." Joe talked very rapidly and always tumbled over his English. He seldom spoke it to his customers, and had never learned much.

Nils swung himself into the saddle and trotted to the west end of the village, where the houses and gardens scattered into prairie-land and the road turned south. Far ahead of him, in the declining light, he saw Clara Vavrika's slender figure, loitering on horseback. He touched his mare with the whip, and shot along the white, level road, under the reddening sky. When he overtook Olaf's wife he saw that she had been crying. "What's the matter, Clara Vavrika?" he asked kindly.

"Oh, I get blue sometimes. It was awfully jolly living there with father. I wonder why I ever went away."

Nils spoke in a low, kind tone that he sometimes used with women: "That's what I've been wondering these many years. You were the last girl in the country I'd have picked for a wife for Olaf. What made you do it, Clara?"

"I suppose I really did it to oblige the neighbors"—Clara tossed her head. "People were beginning to wonder."

"To wonder?"

"Yes—why I didn't get married. I suppose I didn't like to keep them in suspense. I've discovered that most girls marry out of consideration for the neighborhood."

Nils bent his head toward her and his white teeth flashed. "I'd have gambled that one girl I knew would say, 'Let the neighborhood be damned.' "

Clara shook her head mournfully. "You see, they have it on you, Nils; that is, if you're a woman. They say you're beginning to go off. That's what makes us get married: we can't stand the laugh."

Nils looked sideways at her. He had never seen her head droop before. Resignation was the last thing he would have expected of her. "In your case, there wasn't something else?"

"Something else?"

"I mean, you didn't do it to spite somebody? Somebody who didn't come back?"

Clara drew herself up. "Oh, I never thought you'd come back. Not after I stopped writing to you, at least. *That* was all over, long before I married Olaf."

"It never occurred to you, then, that the meanest thing you could do to me was marry Olaf?"

Clara laughed. "No; I didn't know you were so fond of Olaf."

Nils smoothed his horse's mane with his glove. "You know, Clara Vavrika, you are never going to stick it out. You'll cut away some day, and I've been thinking you might as well cut away with me."

Clara threw up her chin. "Oh, you don't know me as well as you think. I won't cut away. Sometimes, when I'm with father, I feel like it. But I can hold out as long as the Ericsons can. They've never got the best of me yet, and one can live, so long as one isn't beaten. If I go back to father, it's all up with Olaf in politics. He knows that, and he never goes much beyond sulking. I've as much wit as the Ericsons. I'll never leave them unless I can show them a thing or two."

"You mean unless you can come it over them?"

"Yes—unless I go away with a man who is cleverer than they are, and who has more money."

Nils whistled. "Dear me, you are demanding a good

deal. The Ericsons, take the lot of them, are a bunch to beat. But I should think the excitement of tormenting them would have worn off by this time."

"It has, I'm afraid," Clara admitted mournfully.

"Then why don't you cut away? There are more amusing games than this in the world. When I came home I thought it might amuse me to bully a few quarter sections out of the Ericsons; but I've almost decided I can get more fun for my money somewhere else."

Clara took in her breath sharply. "Ah, you have got the other will! That was why you came home!"

"No, it wasn't. I came home to see how you were getting on with Olaf."

Clara struck her horse with the whip, and in a bound she was far ahead of him. Nils dropped one word, "Damn!" and whipped after her; but she leaned forward in her saddle and fairly cut the wind. Her long riding-skirt rippled in the still air behind her. The sun was just sinking behind the stubble in a vast, clear sky, and the shadows drew across the fields so rapidly that Nils could scarcely keep in sight the dark figure on the road. When he overtook her he caught her horse by the bridle. Norman reared, and Nils was frightened for her; but Clara kept her seat.

"Let me go, Nils Ericson!" she cried. "I hate you more than any of them. You were created to torture me, the whole tribe of you—to make me suffer in every possible way."

She struck her horse again and galloped away from him. Nils set his teeth and looked thoughtful. He rode slowly home along the deserted road, watching the stars come out in the clear violet sky. They flashed softly into the limpid heavens, like jewels let fall into clear water. They were a reproach, he felt, to a sordid world. As he turned across the sand creek, he looked up at the North Star and smiled, as if there were an understanding between them. His mother scolded him for being late for supper.

V

On Sunday afternoon Joe Vavrika, in his shirt-sleeves and carpet-slippers, was sitting in his garden, smoking a long-tasseled porcelain pipe with a hunting scene painted on the bowl. Clara sat under the cherry tree, reading aloud to him from the weekly Bohemian papers. She had worn a white muslin dress under her riding-habit, and the leaves of the cherry tree threw a pattern of sharp shadows over her skirt. The black cat was dozing in the sunlight at her feet, and Joe's dachshund was scratching a hole under the scarlet geraniums and dreaming of badgers. Joe was filling his pipe for the third time since dinner, when he heard a knocking on the fence. He broke into a loud guffaw and unlatched the little door that led into the street. He did not call Nils by name, but caught him by the hand and dragged him in. Clara stiffened and the color deepened under her dark skin. Nils, too, felt a little awkward. He had not seen her since the night when she rode away from him and left him alone on the level road between the fields. Joe dragged him to the wooden bench beside the green table.

"You bring de flute," he cried, tapping the leather case

under Nils' arm. "Ah, das-a good! Now we have some liddle fun like old times. I got somet'ing good for you." Joe shook his finger at Nils and winked his blue eye, a bright clear eye, full of fire, though the tiny blood-vessels on the ball were always a little distended. "I got somet'ing for you from"—he paused and waved his hand—"Hongarie. You know Hongarie? You wait!" He pushed Nils down on the bench, and went through the back door of his saloon.

Nils looked at Clara, who sat frigidly with her white skirts drawn tight about her. "He didn't tell you he had asked me to come, did he? He wanted a party and proceeded to arrange it. Isn't he fun? Don't be cross; let's give him a good time."

Clara smiled and shook out her skirt. "Isn't that like father? And he has sat here so meekly all day. Well, I won't pout. I'm glad you came. He doesn't have very many good times now any more. There are so few of his kind left. The second generation are a tame lot."

Joe came back with a flask in one hand and three wine-glasses caught by the stems between the fingers of the other. These he placed on the table with an air of ceremony, and, going behind Nils, held the flask between him and the sun, squinting into it admiringly. "You know dis, Tokai? A great friend of mine, he bring dis to me, a present out of Hongarie. You know how much it cost, dis wine? Chust so much what it weigh in gold. Nobody but de nobles drink him in Bohemie. Many, many years I save him up, dis Tokai." Joe whipped out his official corkscrew and delicately removed the cork. "De old man die what bring him to me, an' dis wine he lay on his belly in my cellar an' sleep. An' now," carefully pouring out the heavy yellow wine, "an' now he wake up; and maybe he wake us up, too!" He carried one of the glasses to his daughter and presented it with great gallantry.

Clara shook her head, but, seeing her father's disappointment, relented. "You taste it first. I don't want so much."

Joe sampled it with a beatific expression, and turned to Nils. "You drink him slow, dis wine. He very soft, but he go down hot. You see!"

After a second glass Nils declared that he couldn't take any more without getting sleepy. "Now get your fiddle, Vavrika," he said as he opened his flute-case.

But Joe settled back in his wooden rocker and wagged his big carpet-slipper. "No-no-no-no-no-no-no! No play fiddle now any more: too much ache in de finger," waving them, "all-a-time rheumatiz. You play de flute, te-tety-te-tety-te. Bohemie songs."

"I've forgotten all the Bohemian songs I used to play with you and Johanna. But here's one that will make Clara pout. You remember how her eyes used to snap when we called her the Bohemian Girl?" Nils lifted his flute and began "When Other Lips and Other Hearts," and Joe hummed the air in a husky baritone, waving his carpet-slipper. "Oh-h-h, das-a fine music," he cried, clapping his hands as Nils finished. "Now 'Marble Halls, Marble Halls'! Clara, you sing him."

Clara smiled and leaned back in her chair, beginning softly:

"I dreamt that I dwelt in ma-a-arble halls,
With vassals and serfs at my knee,"

and Joe hummed like a big bumble-bee.

"There's one more you always played," Clara said quietly; "I remember that best." She locked her hands over her knee and began "The Heart Bowed Down," and sang it through without groping for the words. She was singing with a good deal of warmth when she came to the end of the old song:

"For memory is the only friend
That grief can call its own."

Joe flashed out his red silk handkerchief and blew his nose, shaking his head. "No-no-no-no-no-no-no! Too sad, too sad! I not like-a dat. Play quick somet'ing gay now."

Nils put his lips to the instrument, and Joe lay back in his chair, laughing and singing. "Oh, Evelina, Sweet Evelina!" Clara laughed, too. Long ago, when she and Nils went to high school, the model student of their class was a very homely girl in thick spectacles. Her name was Evelina Oleson; she had a long, swinging walk which somehow suggested the measure of that song, and they used mercilessly to sing it at her."

"Dat ugly Oleson girl, she teach in de school," Joe gasped, "an' she still walk chust like dat, yup-a, yup-a, yup-a, chust like a camel she go! Now, Nils, we have some more li'l drink. Oh, yes-yes-yes-yes-yes-yes-*yes*! Dis time you haf to drink, and Clara she haf to, so she show she not jealous.

So, we all drink to your girl. You not tell her name, eh? No-no-no, I no make you tell. She pretty, eh? She make good sweetheart? I bet!" Joe winked and lifted his glass. "How soon you get married?"

Nils screwed up his eyes. "That I don't know. When she says."

Joe threw out his chest. "Das-a way boys talks. No way for mans. Mans say, 'You come to de church, an' get a hurry on you.' Das-a way mans talks."

"Maybe Nils hasn't got enough to keep a wife," put in Clara ironically. "How about that, Nils?" she asked him frankly, as if she wanted to know.

Nils looked at her coolly, raising one eyebrow. "Oh, I can keep her, all right."

"The way she wants to be kept?"

"With my wife, I'll decide that," replied Nils calmly. "I'll give her what's good for her."

Clara made a wry face. "You'll give her the strap, I expect, like old Peter Oleson gave his wife."

"When she needs it," said Nils lazily, locking his hands behind his head and squinting up through the leaves of the cherry tree. "Do you remember the time I squeezed the cherries all over your clean dress, and Aunt Johanna boxed my ears for me? My gracious, weren't you mad! You had both hands full of cherries, and I squeezed 'em and made the juice fly all over you. I liked to have fun with you; you'd get so mad."

"We *did* have fun, didn't we? None of the other kids ever had so much fun. We knew how to play."

Nils dropped his elbows on the table and looked steadily

across at her. "I've played with lots of girls since, but I haven't found one who was such good fun."

Clara laughed. The late afternoon sun was shining full in her face, and deep in the back of her eyes there shone something fiery, like the yellow drops of Tokai in the brown glass bottle. "Can you still play, or are you only pretending?"

"I can play better than I used to, and harder."

"Don't you ever work, then?" She had not intended to say it. It slipped out because she was confused enough to say just the wrong thing.

"I work between times." Nils' steady gaze still beat upon her. "Don't you worry about my working, Mrs. Ericson. You're getting like all the rest of them." He reached his brown, warm hand across the table and dropped it on Clara's, which was cold as an icicle. "Last call for play, Mrs. Ericson!" Clara shivered, and suddenly her hands and cheeks grew warm. Her fingers lingered in his a moment, and they looked at each other earnestly. Joe Vavrika had put the mouth of the bottle to his lips and was swallowing the last drops of the Tokai, standing. The sun, just about to sink behind his shop, glistened on the bright glass, on his flushed face and curly yellow hair. "Look," Clara whispered; "that's the way I want to grow old."

VI

On the day of Olaf Ericson's barn-raising, his wife, for once in a way, rose early. Johanna Vavrika had been baking cakes and frying and boiling and spicing meats for a week beforehand, but it was not until the day before the party was to take place that Clara showed any interest in it. Then she was seized with one of her fitful spasms of energy, and took the wagon and little Eric and spent the day on Plum Creek, gathering vines and swamp goldenrod to decorate the barn.

By four o'clock in the afternoon buggies and wagons began to arrive at the big unpainted building in front of Olaf's house. When Nils and his mother came at five, there were more than fifty people in the barn, and a great drove of children. On the ground floor stood six long tables, set with the crockery of seven flourishing Ericson families, lent for the occasion. In the middle of each table was a big yellow pumpkin, hollowed out and filled with woodbine. In one corner of the barn, behind a pile of green-and-white-striped watermelons, was a circle of chairs for the old people; the younger guests sat on bushel measures or barbed-wire spools, and the children tumbled about in the haymow. The box-stalls Clara had converted into booths. The framework was hidden by goldenrod and sheaves of wheat, and the partitions were covered with wild grape-vines full of fruit. At one of these Johanna Vavrika watched over her cooked meats, enough to provision an army; and at the next her kitchen girls had ranged the ice-cream freezers, and Clara was already cutting pies and cakes against the hour of serving. At the third stall, little Hilda, in a bright pink lawn dress, dispensed lemonade throughout the afternoon. Olaf, as a public man, had thought it inadvisable to serve beer in his barn; but Joe Vavrika had come over with two demijohns concealed in his buggy, and after his arrival the wagon-shed was much frequented by the men.

"Hasn't Cousin Clara fixed things lovely?" little Hilda whispered, when Nils went up to her stall and asked for lemonade.

Nils leaned against the booth, talking to the excited little girl and watching the people. The barn faced the west, and the sun, pouring in at the big doors, filled the whole interior with a golden light, through which filtered fine particles of dust from the haymow, where the children were romping. There was a great chattering from the stall where Johanna Vavrika exhibited to the admiring women her platters heaped with fried chicken, her roasts of beef, boiled tongues, and baked hams with cloves stuck in the crisp brown fat and garnished with tansy and parsley. The older women, having assured themselves that there were twenty kinds of cake, not counting cookies, and three dozen fat pies, repaired to the corner behind the pile of watermelons, put on their white aprons, and fell to their knitting and fancy-work. They were a fine company of old women, and a Dutch painter would have loved to find them there together, where the sun made bright patches on the floor and sent long, quivering shafts of gold through the dusky shade up among the rafters. There were fat, rosy old women who looked hot in their best black dresses; spare, alert old women with brown, dark-veined hands; and several of almost heroic frame, not less massive than old Mrs. Ericson herself. Few of them wore glasses, and old Mrs. Svendsen, a Danish woman, who was quite bald, wore the only cap among them. Mrs. Oleson, who had twelve big grandchildren, could still show two braids of yellow hair as thick as her own wrists. Among all these grandmothers there were more brown heads than white.

They all had a pleased, properous air, as if they were more than satisfied with themselves and with life. Nils, leaning against Hilda's lemonade-stand, watched them as they sat chattering in four languages, their fingers never lagging behind their tongues.

"Look at them over there," he whispered, detaining Clara as she passed him. "Aren't they the Old Guard? I've just counted thirty hands. I guess they've wrung many a chicken's neck and warmed many a boy's jacket for him in their time."

In reality he fell into amazement when he thought of the Herculean labors those fifteen pairs of hands had performed: of the cows they had milked, the butter they had made, the gardens they had planted, the children and grandchildren they had tended, the brooms they had worn out, the mountains of food they had cooked. It made him dizzy. Clara Vavrika smiled a hard, enigmatical smile at him and walked rapidly away. Nils' eyes followed her white figure as she went toward the house. He watched her walking alone in the sunlight, looked at her slender, defiant shoulders and her little hard-set head with its coils of blue-black hair. "No," he reflected; "she'd never be like them, not if she lived here a hundred years. She'd only grow more bitter. You can't tame a wild thing; you can only chain it. People aren't all alike. I mustn't lose my nerve." He gave Hilda's pigtail a parting tweak and set out after Clara. "Where to?" he asked, as he came upon her in the kitchen.

"I'm going to the cellar for preserves."

"Let me go with you. I never get a moment alone with you. Why do you keep out of my way?"

Clara laughed. "I don't usually get in anybody's way."

Nils followed her down the stairs and to the far corner of the cellar, where a basement window let in a stream of light. From a swinging shelf Clara selected several glass jars, each labeled in Johanna's careful hand. Nils took up a brown flask. "What's this? It looks good."

"It is. It's some French brandy father gave me when I was married. Would you like some? Have you a corkscrew? I'll get glasses."

When she brought them, Nils took them from her and put them down on the window-sill. "Clara Vavrika, do you remember how crazy I used to be about you?"

Clara shrugged her shoulders. "Boys are always crazy about somebody or other. I dare say some silly has been crazy about Evelina Oleson. You got over it in a hurry."

"Because I didn't come back, you mean? I had to get on, you know, and it was hard sledding at first. Then I heard you'd married Olaf."

"And then you stayed away from a broken heart," Clara laughed.

"And then I began to think about you more than I had since I first went away. I began to wonder if you were really as you had seemed to me when I was a boy. I thought I'd like to see. I've had lots of girls, but no one ever pulled me the same way. The more I thought about you, the more I remembered how it used to be—like hearing a wild tune you can't resist, calling you out at night. It had been a long while since anything had pulled me out of my boots, and I wondered whether anything ever could again." Nils thrust his hands into his coat pockets and squared his shoulders, as his mother sometimes squared hers, as Olaf, in a clumsier manner, squared his. "So I thought I'd come back and see. Of course the family have tried to do me, and I rather thought I'd bring out father's will and make a fuss. But they can have their old land; they've put enough sweat into it." He took the flask and filled the two glasses carefully to the brim. "I've found out what I want from the Ericsons. Drink *skoal*, Clara." He lifted his glass, and Clara took hers with downcast eyes. "Look at me, Clara Vavrika. *Skoal!*"

She raised her burning eyes and answered fiercely: "*Skoal!*"

The barn supper began at six o'clock and lasted for two hilarious hours. Yense Nelson had made a wager that he could eat two whole fried chickens, and he did. Eli Swanson stowed away two whole custard pies, and Nick Hermanson ate a chocolate layer cake to the last crumb. There was even a cooky contest among the children, and one thin, slablike Bohemian boy consumed sixteen and won the prize, a gingerbread pig which Johanna Vavrika had carefully decorated with red candies and burnt sugar. Fritz Sweiheart, the German carpenter, won in the pickle contest, but he disappeared soon after supper and was not seen for the rest of the evening. Joe Vavrika said that Fritz could have managed the pickles all right, but he had sampled the demijohn in his buggy too often before sitting down to the table.

While the supper was being cleared away the two fiddlers began to tune up for the dance. Clara was to accompany them on her old upright piano, which had been brought down from her father's. By this time Nils had renewed old acquaintances. Since his interview with Clara in

78

the cellar, he had been busy telling all the old women how young they looked, and all the young ones how pretty they were, and assuring the men that they had here the best farm-land in the world. He had made himself so agreeable that old Mrs. Ericson's friends began to come up to her and tell how lucky she was to get her smart son back again, and please to get him to play his flute. Joe Vavrika, who could still play very well when he forgot that he had rheumatism, caught up a fiddle from Johnny Oleson and played a crazy Bohemian dance tune that set the wheels going. When he dropped the bow every one was ready to dance.

Olaf, in a frock-coat and a solemn made-up necktie, led the grand march with his mother. Clara had kept well out of *that* by sticking to the piano. She played the march with a pompous solemnity which greatly amused the prodigal son, who went over and stood behind her.

"Oh, aren't you rubbing it into them, Clara Vavrika? And aren't you lucky to have me here, or all your wit would be thrown away."

"I'm used to being witty for myself. It saves my life."

The fiddles struck up a polka, and Nils convulsed Joe Vavrika by leading out Evelina Oleson, the homely school-teacher. His next partner was a very fat Swedish girl, who, although she was an heiress, had not been asked for the first dance, but had stood against the wall in her tight, high-heeled shoes, nervously fingering a lace handkerchief. She was soon out of breath, so Nils led her, pleased and panting, to her seat, and went over to the piano, from which Clara had been watching his gallantry. "Ask Olena Yenson," she whispered. "She waltzes beautifully."

Olena, too, was rather inconveniently plump, handsome in a smooth, heavy way, with a fine color and good-natured, sleepy eyes. She was redolent of violet sachet powder, and had warm, soft, white hands, but she danced divinely, moving as smoothly as the tide coming in. "There, that's something like," Nils said as he released her. "You'll give me the next waltz, won't you? Now I must go and dance with my little cousin."

Hilda was greatly excited when Nils went up to her stall and held out his arm. Her little eyes sparkled, but she declared that she could not leave her lemonade. Old Mrs. Ericson, who happened along at this moment, said she would attend to that, and Hilda came out, as pink as her pink dress. The dance was a schottische, and in a moment her yellow braids were fairly standing on end. "Bravo!" Nils cried encouragingly. "Where did you learn to dance so nicely?"

"My Cousin Clara taught me," the little girl panted.

Nils found Eric sitting with a group of boys who were too awkward or too shy to dance, and told him that he must dance the next waltz with Hilda.

The boy screwed up his shoulders. "Aw, Nils, I can't dance. My feet are too big; I look silly."

"Don't be thinking about yourself. It doesn't matter how boys look."

Nils had never spoken to him so sharply before, and Eric made haste to scramble out of his corner and brush the straw from his coat.

Clara nodded approvingly. "Good for you, Nils. I've

been trying to get hold of him. They dance very nicely together; I sometimes play for them."

"I'm obliged to you for teaching him. There's no reason why he should grow up to be a lout."

"He'll never be that. He's more like you than any of them. Only he hasn't your courage." From her slanting eyes Clara shot forth one of those keen glances, admiring and at the same time challenging, which she seldom bestowed on any one, and which seemed to say, "Yes, I admire you, but I am your equal."

Clara was proving a much better host than Olaf, who, once the supper was over, seemed to feel no interest in anything but the lanterns. He had brought a locomotive headlight from town to light the revels, and he kept skulking about it as if he feared the mere light from it might set his new barn on fire. His wife, on the contrary, was cordial to every one, was animated and even gay. The deep salmon color in her cheeks burned vividly, and her eyes were full of life. She gave the piano over to the fat Swedish heiress, pulled her father away from the corner where he sat gossiping with his cronies, and made him dance a Bohemian dance with her. In his youth Joe had been a famous dancer, and his daughter got him so limbered up that every one sat round and applauded them. The old ladies were particularly delighted, and made them go through the dance again. From their corner where they watched and commented, the old women kept time with their feet and hands, and whenever the fiddles struck up a new air old Mrs. Svendsen's white cap would begin to bob.

Clara was waltzing with little Eric when Nils came up to them, brushed his brother aside, and swung her out among the dancers. "Remember how we used to waltz on rollers at the old skating rink in town? I suppose people don't do that any more. We used to keep it up for hours. You know, we never did moon around as other boys and girls did. It was dead serious with us from the beginning. When we were most in love with each other, we used to fight. You were always pinching people; your fingers were like little nippers. A regular snapping-turtle, you were. Lord, how you'd like Stockholm! Sit out in the streets in front of cafés and talk all night in summer. Just like a reception—officers and ladies and funny English people. Jolliest people in the world, the Swedes, once you get them going. Always drinking things—champagne and stout mixed, half-and-half; serve it out of big pitchers, and serve plenty. Slow pulse, you know; they can stand a lot. Once they light up, they're glow-worms, I can tell you."

"All the same, you don't really like gay people."

"*I* don't?"

"No; I could see that when you were looking at the old women there this afternoon. They're the kind you really admire, after all; women like your mother. And that's the kind you'll marry."

"Is it, Miss Wisdom? You'll see who I'll marry, and she won't have a domestic virtue to bless herself with. She'll be a snapping-turtle, and she'll be a match for me. All the same, they're a fine bunch of old dames over there. You admire them yourself."

"No, I don't; I detest them."

"You won't, when you look back on them from Stockholm or Budapest. Freedom settles all that. Oh, but you're the real Bohemian Girl, Clara Vavrika!" Nils laughed down at her sullen frown and began mockingly to sing:

"Oh, how could a poor gypsy maiden like me
Expect the proud bride of a baron to be?"

Clara clutched his shoulder. "Hush, Nils; every one is looking at you."

"I don't care. They can't gossip. It's all in the family, as the Ericsons say when they divide up little Hilda's patrimony amongst them. Besides, we'll give them something to talk about when we hit the trail. Lord, it will be a godsend to them! They haven't had anything so interesting to chatter about since the grasshopper year. It'll give them a new lease of life. And Olaf won't lose the Bohemian vote, either. They'll have the laugh on him so that they'll vote two apiece. They'll send him to Congress. They'll never forget his barn party, or us. They'll always remember us as we're dancing together now. We're making a legend. Where's my waltz, boys?" he called as they whirled past the fiddlers.

The musicians grinned, looked at each other, hesitated, and began a new air; and Nils sang with them, as the couples fell from a quick waltz to a long, slow glide:

"When other lips and other hearts
Their tale of love shall tell,
In language whose excess imparts
The power they feel so well."

The old women applauded vigorously. "What a gay one he is, that Nils!" And old Mrs. Svendsen's cap lurched dreamily from side to side to the flowing measure of the dance.

"Of days that have as ha-a-p-py been,
And you'll remember me."

VII

———

The moonlight flooded that great, silent land. The reaped fields lay yellow in it. The straw stacks and poplar wind-breaks threw sharp black shadows. The roads were white rivers of dust. The sky was a deep, crystalline blue, and the stars were few and faint. Everything seemed to have succumbed, to have sunk to sleep, under the great, golden, tender, midsummer moon. The splendor of it seemed to transcend human life and human fate. The senses were too feeble to take it in, and every time one looked up at the sky one felt unequal to it, as if one were sitting deaf under the waves of a great river of melody. Near the road, Nils Ericson was lying against a straw stack in Olaf's wheat-field. His own life seemed strange and unfamiliar to him, as if it were something he had read about, or dreamed, and forgotten. He lay very still, watching the white road that ran in front of him, lost itself among the fields, and then, at a distance, reappeared over a little hill. At last, against this white band he saw something moving rapidly, and he got up and walked to the edge of the field. "She is passing the row of poplars now," he thought. He heard the padded beat of hoofs along the dusty road, and as she came into sight he stepped out and waved his arms. Then, for fear of frightening the horse, he drew back and waited. Clara had seen him, and she came up at a walk. Nils took the horse by the bit and stroked his neck.

"What are you doing out so late, Clara Vavrika? I went to the house but Johanna told me you had gone to your father's."

"Who can stay in the house on a night like this? Aren't you out yourself?"

"Ah, but that's another matter."

Nils turned the horse into the field.

"What are you doing? Where are you taking Norman?"

"Not far, but I want to talk to you to-night; I have something to say to you. I can't talk to you at the house, with Olaf sitting there on the porch, weighing a thousand tons."

Clara laughed. "He won't be sitting there now. He's in bed by this time, and asleep—weighing a thousand tons."

Nils plodded on across the stubble. "Are you really going to spend the rest of your life like this, night after night, summer after summer? Haven't you anything better to do on a night like this than to wear yourself and Norman out tearing across the country to your father's and back? Besides, your father won't live forever, you know. His little place will be shut up or sold, and then you'll have nobody but the Ericsons. You'll have to fasten down the hatches for the winter then."

Clara moved her head restlessly. "Don't talk about that.

I try never to think of it. If I lost father I'd lose everything, even my hold over the Ericsons."

"Bah! You'd lose a good deal more than that. You'd lose your race, everything that makes you yourself. You've lost a good deal of it now."

"Of what?"

"Of your love of life, your capacity for delight."

Clara put her hands up to her face. "I haven't, Nils Ericson, I haven't! Say anything to me but that. I won't have it!" she declared vehemently.

Nils led the horse up to a straw stack, and turned to Clara, looking at her intently, as he had looked at her that Sunday afternoon at Vavrika's. "But why do you fight for that so? What good is the power to enjoy, if you never enjoy? Your hands are cold again; what are you afraid of all the time? Ah, you're afraid of losing it; that's what's the matter with you! And you will, Clara Vavrika, you will! When I used to know you—listen; you've caught a wild bird in your hand, haven't you, and felt its heart beat so hard that you were afraid it would shatter its little body to pieces? Well, you used to be just like that, a slender, eager thing with a wild delight inside you. That is how I remembered you. And I come back and find you—a bitter woman. This is a perfect ferret fight here; you live by biting and being bitten. Can't you remember what life used to be? Can't you remember that old delight? I've never forgotten it, or known its like, on land or sea."

He drew the horse under the shadow of the straw stack. Clara felt him take her foot out of the stirrup, and she slid softly down into his arms. He kissed her slowly. He was a deliberate man, but his nerves were steel when he wanted anything. Something flashed out from him like a knife out of a sheath. Clara felt everything slipping away from her; she was flooded by the summer night. He thrust his hand into his pocket, and then held it out at arm's length. "Look," he said. The shadow of the straw stack fell sharp across his wrist, and in the palm of his hand she saw a silver dollar shining. "That's my pile," he muttered; "will you go with me?"

Clara nodded, and dropped her forehead on his shoulder. Nils took a deep breath. "Will you go with me to-night?"

"Where?" she whispered softly.

"To town, to catch the midnight flyer."

Clara lifted her head and pulled herself together. "Are you crazy, Nils? We couldn't go away like that."

"That's the only way we ever will go. You can't sit on the bank and think about it. You have to plunge. That's the way I've always done, and it's the right way for people like you and me. There's nothing so dangerous as sitting still. You've only got one life, one youth, and you can let it slip through your fingers if you want to; nothing easier. Most people do that. You'd be better off tramping the roads with me than you are here." Nils held back her head and looked into her eyes. "But I'm not that kind of a tramp, Clara. You won't have to take in sewing. I'm with a Norwegian shipping line; came over on business with the New York offices, but now I'm going straight back to Bergen. I expect I've got as much money as the Ericsons. Father sent me a little to get started. They never knew about that. There, I hadn't meant to tell you; I wanted you to come on your own nerve."

Clara looked off across the fields. "It isn't that, Nils, but something seems to hold me. I'm afraid to pull against it. It comes out of the ground, I think."

"I know all about that. One has to tear loose. You're not needed here. Your father will understand; he's made like us. As for Olaf, Johanna will take better care of him than ever you could. It's now or never, Clara Vavrika. My bag's at the station; I smuggled it there yesterday."

Clara clung to him and hid her face against his shoulder. "Not to-night," she whispered. "Sit here and talk to me tonight. I don't want to go anywhere to-night. I may never love you like this again."

Nils laughed through his teeth. "You can't come that on me. That's not my way, Clara Vavrika. Eric's mare is over there behind the stacks, and I'm off on the midnight. It's good-bye, or off across the world with me. My carriage won't wait. I've written a letter to Olaf; I'll mail it in town. When he reads it he won't bother us—not if I know him. He'd rather have the land. Besides, I could demand an investigation of his administration of Cousin Henrik's estate, and that would be bad for a public man. You've no clothes, I know; but you can sit up tonight, and we can get everything on the way. Where's your old dash, Clara Vavrika? What's become of your Bohemian blood? I used to think you had courage enough for anything. Where's your nerve—what are you waiting for?"

Clara drew back her head, and he saw the slumberous fire in her eyes. "For you to say one thing, Nils Ericson."

"I never say that thing to any woman, Clara Vavrika."

He leaned back, lifted her gently from the ground, and whispered through his teeth: "But I'll never, never let you go, not to any man on earth but me! Do you understand me? Now, wait here."

Clara sank down on a sheaf of wheat and covered her face with her hands. She did not know what she was going to do—whether she would go or stay. The great, silent country seemed to lay a spell upon her. The ground seemed to hold her as if by roots. Her knees were soft under her. She felt as if she could not bear separation from her old sorrows, from her old discontent. They were dear to her, they had kept her alive, they were a part of her. There would be nothing left of her if she were wrenched away from them. Never could she pass beyond that sky-line against which her restlessness had beat so many times. She felt as if her soul had built itself a nest there on that horizon at which she looked every morning and every evening, and it was dear to her, inexpressibly dear. She pressed her fingers against her eyeballs to shut it out. Beside her she heard the tramping of horses in the soft earth. Nils said nothing to her. He put his hands under her arms and lifted her lightly to her saddle. Then he swung himself into his own.

"We shall have to ride fast to catch the midnight train. A last gallop, Clara Vavrika. Forward!"

There was a start, a thud of hoofs along the moonlit road, two dark shadows going over the hill; and then the great, still land stretched untroubled under the azure night. Two shadows had passed.

VIII

A year after the flight of Olaf Ericson's wife, the night train was steaming across the plains of Iowa. The conductor was hurrying through one of the day-coaches, his lantern on his arm, when a lank, fair-haired boy sat up in one of the plush seats and tweaked him by the coat.

"What is the next stop, please, sir?"

"Red Oak, Iowa. But you go through to Chicago, don't you?" He looked down, and noticed that the boy's eyes were red and his face was drawn, as if he were in trouble.

"Yes. But I was wondering whether I could get off at the next place and get a train back to Omaha."

"Well, I suppose you could. Live in Omaha?"

"No. In the western part of the State. How soon do we get to Red Oak?"

"Forty minutes. You'd better make up your mind, so I can tell the baggageman to put your trunk off."

"Oh, never mind about that! I mean, I haven't got any," the boy added, blushing.

"Run away," the conductor thought, as he slammed the coach door behind him.

Eric Ericson crumpled down in his seat and put his brown hand to his forehead. He had been crying, and he had had no supper, and his head was aching violently. "Oh, what shall I do?" he thought, as he looked dully down at his big shoes. "Nils will be ashamed of me; I haven't got any spunk."

Ever since Nils had run away with his brother's wife, life at home had been hard for little Eric. His mother and Olaf both suspected him of complicity. Mrs. Ericson was harsh and fault-finding, constantly wounding the boy's pride; and Olaf was always setting her against him.

Joe Vavrika heard often from his daughter. Clara had always been fond of her father, and happiness made her kinder. She wrote him long accounts of the voyage to Bergen, and of the trip she and Nils took through Bohemia to the little town where her father had grown up and where she herself was born. She visited all her kinsmen there, and sent her father news of his brother, who was a priest; of his sister, who had married a horse-breeder—of their big farm and their many children. These letters Joe always managed to read to little Eric. They contained messages for Eric and Hilda. Clara sent presents, too, which Eric never dared to take home and which poor little Hilda never even saw, though she loved to hear Eric tell about them when they were out getting the eggs together. But Olaf once saw Eric coming out of Vavrika's house,—the old man had never asked the boy to come into his saloon,—and Olaf went straight to his mother and told her. That night Mrs. Ericson came to Eric's room after he was in bed and made a terrible scene. She could be very terrifying when she was really angry. She forbade him ever to speak to Vavrika again, and after that night she would not allow him to go to town alone. So it was a long while before Eric got any more news of his brother. But old Joe suspected what was going on, and he carried Clara's letters about in his pocket. One Sunday he drove out to see a German friend of his, and chanced to catch sight of Eric, sitting by the cattle-pond in the big pasture. They went together into Fritz Oberlies' barn, and read the letters and talked things over.

Eric admitted that things were getting hard for him at home. That very night old Joe sat down and laboriously penned a statement of the case to his daughter.

Things got no better for Eric. His mother and Olaf felt that, however closely he was watched, he still, as they said, "heard." Mrs. Ericson could not admit neutrality. She had sent Johanna Vavrika packing back to her brother's, though Olaf would much rather have kept her than Anders' eldest daughter, whom Mrs. Ericson installed in her place. He was not so high-handed as his mother, and he once sulkily told her that she might better have taught her granddaughter to cook before she sent Johanna away. Olaf could have borne a good deal for the sake of prunes spiced in honey, the secret of which Johanna had taken away with her.

At last two letters came to Joe Vavrika: one from Nils, inclosing a postal order for money to pay Eric's passage to Bergen, and one from Clara, saying that Nils had a place for Eric in the offices of his company, that he was to live with them, and that they were only waiting for him to come. He was to leave New York on one of the boats of Nils' own line; the captain was one of their friends, and Eric was to make himself known at once.

Nils' directions were so explicit that a baby could have followed them, Eric felt. And here he was, nearing Red Oak, Iowa, and rocking backward and forward in despair. Never had he loved his brother so much, and never had the big world called to him so hard. But there was a lump in his throat which would not go down. Ever since nightfall he had been tormented by the thought of his mother, alone in that big house that had sent forth so many men. Her unkindness now seemed so little, and her loneliness so great. He remembered everything she had ever done for him: how frightened she had been when he tore his hand in the corn-sheller, and how she wouldn't let Olaf scold him. When Nils went away he didn't leave his mother all alone, or he would never have gone. Eric felt sure of that.

The train whistled. The conductor came in, smiling not unkindly. "Well, young man, what are you going to do? We stop at Red Oak in three minutes."

"Yes, thank you. I'll let you know." The conductor went out, and the boy doubled up with misery. He couldn't let his one chance go like this. He felt for his breast pocket and crackled Nils' kind letter to give him courage. He didn't want Nils to be ashamed of him. The train stopped. Suddenly he remembered his brother's kind, twinkling eyes, that always looked at you as if from far away. The lump in his throat softened. "Ah, but Nils, Nils would *understand!*" he thought. "That's just it about Nils; he always understands."

A lank, pale boy with a canvas telescope stumbled off the train to the Red Oak siding, just as the conductor called, "All aboard!"

The next night Mrs. Ericson was sitting alone in her wooden rocking-chair on the front porch. Little Hilda had been sent to bed and had cried herself to sleep. The old woman's knitting was in her lap, but her hands lay motionless on top of it. For more than an hour she had not moved a muscle. She simply sat, as only the Ericsons and the mountains can sit. The house was dark, and there was no sound but the croaking of the frogs down in the pond of the little pasture.

Eric did not come home by the road, but across the fields, where no one could see him. He set his telescope down softly in the kitchen shed, and slipped noiselessly along the path to the front porch. He sat down on the step without saying anything. Mrs. Ericson made no sign, and the frogs croaked on. At last the boy spoke timidly.

"I've come back, Mother."

"Very well," said Mrs. Ericson.

Eric leaned over and picked up a little stick out of the grass.

"How about the milking?" he faltered.

"That's been done, hours ago."

"Who did you get?"

"Get? I did it myself. I can milk as good as any of you."

Eric slid along the step nearer to her. "Oh, Mother, why did you?" he asked sorrowfully. "Why didn't you get one of Otto's boys?"

"I didn't want anybody to know I was in need of a boy," said Mrs. Ericson bitterly. She looked straight in front of her and her mouth tightened. "I always meant to give you the home farm," she added.

The boy started and slid closer. "Oh, Mother," he faltered, "I don't care about the farm. I came back because I thought you might be needing me, maybe." He hung his head and got no further.

"Very well," said Mrs. Ericson. Her hand went out from her suddenly and rested on his head. Her fingers twined themselves in his soft, pale hair. His tears splashed down on the boards; happiness filled his heart.

A GOLD SLIPPER

MARSHALL McKANN followed his wife and her friend Mrs. Post down the aisle and up the steps to the stage of the Carnegie Music Hall with an ill-concealed feeling of grievance. Heaven knew he never went to concerts, and to be mounted upon the stage in this fashion, as if he were a crank from Sewickley, or some unfortunate with a musical wife, was ludicrous. A man went to concerts when he was courting, while he was a junior partner. When he became a person of substance he stopped that sort of nonsense. His wife, too, was a sensible person, the daughter of an old Pittsburgh family as solid and well-rooted as the McKanns. She would never have bothered him about this concert had not the meddlesome Mrs. Post arrived to pay her a visit. Mrs. Post was an old school friend of Mrs. McKann, and because she lived in Cincinnati she was always keeping up with the world and talking about things in which no one else was interested, music among them. She was an aggressive lady, with weighty opinions, and a deep voice like a jovial bassoon. She had arrived only last night, and at dinner she brought it out that she could on no account miss Kitty Ayrshire's recital; it was, she said, the sort of thing one couldn't afford to miss.

When McKann went into town in the morning he found

that every seat in the music-hall was sold. He telephoned his wife to that effect, and, thinking he had settled the matter, made his reservation on the 11.25 train for New York. He was unable to get a drawing-room because this same Kitty Ayrshire had taken the last one. He had not intended going to New York until the following week, but he preferred to be absent during Mrs. Post's incumbency.

In the middle of the morning, when he was deep in his correspondence, his wife called him up to say the enterprising Mrs. Post had telephoned some musical friends in Sewickley and had found that two hundred folding-chairs were to be placed on the stage of the concert-hall, behind the piano, and that they would be on sale at noon. Would he please get seats in the front row? McKann asked if they would not excuse him, since he was going over to New York on the late train, would be tired, and would not have time to dress, etc. No, not at all. It would be foolish for two women to trail up to the stage unattended. Mrs. Post's husband always accompanied her to concerts, and she expected that much attention from her host. He needn't dress, and he could take a taxi from the concert-hall to the East Liberty station.

The outcome of it all was that, though his bag was at the station, here was McKann, in the worst possible humor, facing the large audience to which he was well known, and sitting among a lot of music students and excitable old maids. Only the desperately zealous or the morbidly curious would endure two hours in those wooden chairs, and he sat in the front row of this hectic body, somehow made a party to a transaction for which he had the utmost contempt.

When McKann had been in Paris, Kitty Ayrshire was singing at the Comique, and he wouldn't go to hear her—even there, where one found so little that was better to do. She was too much talked about, too much advertised; always being thrust in an American's face as if she were something to be proud of. Perfumes and petticoats and cutlets were named for her. Some one had pointed Kitty out to him one afternoon when she was driving in the Bois with a French composer—old enough, he judged, to be her father—who was said to be infatuated, overwhelmed with her, and had told him that this was one of the historic passions of old age. McKann had looked at her, but she was so befrilled and befeathered that he caught nothing but a graceful outline and a small, dark head above a white ostrich boa. He noted with disgust the stooped shoulders and white imperial of the silk-hatted man beside her, and the senescent line of his back. McKann had told his wife about this unpleasing sight the night before, while he was undressing, when he was making every possible effort to avert this concert party. But Bessie only looked superior and said she wished to hear Kitty Ayrshire sing, and that her "private life" was something in which she had no interest.

Well, here he was, hot and uncomfortable, in a chair much too small for him, with a row of blinding footlights glaring in his eyes. Suddenly the door at his right elbow opened. Their seats were at one end of the front row; he had thought they would be less conspicuous there than in the center, and he had not foreseen that the singer would walk over him every time she came upon the stage. Her velvet train brushed against his trousers as she passed him.

The applause which greeted her was neither overwhelming nor prolonged. Her conservative audience did not know exactly how to accept her toilette. They were accustomed to dignified concert gowns, like those which Pittsburgh matrons wore at their daughters' coming-out tea. Kitty's gown that evening was really quite outrageous—the repartee of a conscienceless Parisian designer who took her hint that she wished something that would be entirely novel in the States. To-day, after we have all of us, even in the uttermost provinces, been educated by Baskt and the various Ballets Russes, we would accept such a gown without distrust; but then it was a little disconcerting, even to the well-disposed. It was constructed of a yard or two of green velvet—a reviling, shrieking green which would have made a fright of any woman who had not inextinguishable beauty—and it was made without armholes, a device to which we were then so unaccustomed that it was nothing less than alarming. The velvet skirt split back from a transparent gold-lace petticoat, gold stockings, gold slippers. The narrow train was, apparently, looped to both ankles, and it kept curling about her feet like a serpent's tail, turning up its gold lining as if it were squirming over on its back. It was not, we felt, a costume in which to sing Mozart and Handel and Beethoven. Kitty felt the chill in the air, and it amused her. She liked to be thought a brilliant artist by other artists, but by the world at large she liked to be thought a daring creature. She had every reason to believe, from experience and from example, that to shock the great crowd was the surest way to get its money and to make her name a household word. Nobody ever became a household word by being an artist, surely, and you were not a thoroughly paying proposition until your name meant something on the sidewalk and in the barber-shop. Kitty studied her audience with an appraising eye. She liked the stimulus of this disapprobation. There was some zest about getting through to a hard-shelled public. She felt keen and interested; she knew that she would give such a recital as cannot often be heard for money. She nodded gaily to the young man at the piano, fell into an attitude of seriousness, and began the group of Beethoven and Mozart songs.

Though McKann would not have admitted it, there were really a great many people in the concert-hall who knew what the prodigal daughter of their country was singing, and how well she was doing it. They thawed gradually under the beauty of her voice and the subtlety of her interpretation. She had sung seldom in concert then, and they had supposed her very dependent upon the accessories of opera. Clean singing, finished artistry, were not what they expected from her. They began to feel, even, the wayward charm of her personality.

McKann, who stared coldly up at the balconies during her first song, during the second began to glance cautiously at the green apparition before him. He was vexed with her for having retained a débutante figure. He comfortably classed all singers—especially operatic singers—as "fat Dutchwomen" or "shifty Sadies," and Kitty would not fit into his clever generalization. She displayed, under his nose, the only kind of figure he considered worth looking at—that of a very young girl, supple and sinuous and quicksilverish; thin, eager shoulders, polished white arms that were nowhere too fat and nowhere too thin. McKann found it agreeable to look at Kitty, but when he saw that the authoritative Mrs. Post, red as a turkey-cock with opinions she was bursting to impart, was studying and appraising the singer through her lorgnette, he looked indifferently out into the house again. He felt for his watch, but his wife touched him warningly with her elbow—which he noticed was not at all like Kitty's.

When Miss Ayrshire finished her first group of songs, her audience expressed its approval positively, but guardedly. She smiled bewitchingly upon the people in front of her, glanced up at the balconies, and then turned to the company huddled on the stage behind her. After her gay and careless bows, she retreated toward the stage door. As she passed McKann, she again brushed lightly against him, and this time she paused long enough to glance down at him and murmur, "Pardon." In the moment her bright, curious eyes rested upon him McKann seemed to see himself as if she were holding a mirror up before him. He beheld himself a heavy, solid figure, unsuitably clad for the time and place, with a florid, square face, well-vizored with good living and sane opinions—an inexpressive countenance. Not a rock face, exactly, but a kind of pressed-brick-and-cement face, a "business" face upon which years and feelings had made no mark—in which cocktails might eventually blast out a few hollows. He had never seen himself so distinctly in his shaving-glass as he did in that instant when Kitty Ayrshire's liquid eye held him, when her bright, inquiring glance roamed over his person. When her prehensile train curled over his boot and she was gone, his wife turned to him and said in the tone of approbation one uses when an infant manifests its groping intelligence, "Very gracious of her, I'm sure." Mrs. Post nodded oracularly. McKann grunted.

Kitty began her second number, a group of romantic German songs which were altogether more her affair than her first number. When she turned once to acknowledge the applause behind her, she caught McKann in the act of yawning behind his hand—he of course wore no gloves— and he thought she frowned a little. This did not embarrass him, but it somehow made him feel important. When she retired after the second part of the programme, she again looked him over curiously as she passed, and she took marked precaution that her dress did not touch him. Mrs. Post and his wife again remarked upon her consideration.

The final number was made up of modern French songs which Kitty sang enchantingly, and at last had her way with her frigid public. While she was coming back again and again to smile and curtsy, McKann whispered to his wife that if there were to be encores he had better make a dash for his train.

"Not at all," put in Mrs. Post. "Kitty is going on the same train. She sings in 'Faust' at the opera to-morrow night, so she'll take no chances."

McKann once more told himself how sorry he felt for Post. At last Miss Ayrshire returned, escorted by her accompanist, and gave the people what she of course knew they wanted, the most popular aria from the French opera of which the title-rôle had become synonymous with her name—an opera written for her and to her and round about her by the veteran French composer who so much admired her, the last and not the palest flash of his creative fire. This brought her audience all the way. They clamored for more of it, but she was not to be coerced. She had been unyielding through storms to which this was a summer breeze. She came on once more, shrugged her shoulders, blew them a kiss, and was gone. Her last smile was for that uncomfortable part of her audience seated behind her, and she looked with recognition at McKann and his ladies as she nodded good night to the wooden chairs.

McKann hurried his charges into the foyer by the nearest exit and put them into his motor. Then he went over to the Schenley to have a glass of beer and a rarebit before train time. He had not, he admitted to himself, been so much bored as he pretended. The minx herself was well enough, but it was absurd in his fellow-townsmen to look owlish and uplifted about her. He had no rooted dislike for pretty women; he even didn't deny that gay girls had their place in the world, but they ought to be kept in their place. He was born a Presbyterian, just as he was born a McKann. He sat in his pew in the First Church every Sunday, and he never missed a presbytery meeting when he was in town. His religion was not very spiritual, certainly, but it was substantial and concrete, made up of good, hard convictions and opinions. It had something to do with citizenship, with whom one ought to marry, with the coal business, in which his own name was powerful, with the Republican party, and with all majorities and established precedents. He was hostile to fads, to enthusiasms, to individualism, to all changes except in mining machinery and in methods of transportation.

His equanimity restored by his lunch at the Schenley, McKann lit a big cigar, got into his taxi, and bowled off through the sleet. There was not a sound to be heard or a light to be seen. The ice glittered on the pavement and on the naked trees. No restless feet were abroad. At eleven o'clock the rows of small, comfortable houses looked as empty of the troublesome bubble of life as the Allegheny cemetery itself. Suddenly the cab stopped, and McKann thrust his head out of the window. A woman was standing in the middle of the street addressing his driver in a tone of excitement. Over against the curb a lone electric stood despondent in the storm. The young woman, her cloak blowing about her, turned from the driver to McKann himself, speaking rapidly and somewhat incoherently.

"Could you not be so kind as to help us? It is Mees Ayrshire, the singer. The juice is gone out and we cannot move. We must get to the station. Mademoiselle cannot miss the train; she sings to-morrow night in New York. It is very important. Could you not take us to the station at East Liberty?"

McKann opened the door. "That's all right, but you'll have to hurry. It's eleven-ten now. You've only got fifteen minutes to make the train. Tell her to come along."

The maid drew back and looked up at him in amazement. "But, the hand-luggage to carry, and Mademoiselle to walk! The street is like glass!"

McKann threw away his cigar and followed her. He

stood silent by the door of the derelict, while the maid explained that she had found help. Miss Ayrshire seemed not at all apprehensive; she had not doubted that a rescuer would be forthcoming. She moved deliberately; out of a whirl of skirts she thrust one fur-topped shoe—McKann saw the flash of the gold stocking above it by the street lamp—and alighted. "So kind of you! So fortunate for us!" she murmured. One hand she placed upon his sleeve, and with the other she guarded an armful of roses that had been sent up to the concert stage. The petals showered upon the sooty, sleety pavement as she picked her way along. They would be lying there to-morrow morning, and the children in those houses would wonder if there had been a funeral. The maid followed with two leather bags. As soon as he had lifted Kitty into his cab she exclaimed:

"My jewel-case! I have forgotten it. It is on the back seat, please. I am so careless!"

He dashed back, ran his hand along the cushions, and discovered a small leather bag. When he returned he found the maid and the luggage bestowed on the front seat, and a place left for him on the back seat beside Kitty and her flowers.

"Shall we be taking you far out of your way?" she asked, sweetly. "I haven't an idea where the station is. I'm not even sure about the name. Céline thinks it is East Liberty, but I think it is West Liberty. An odd name, anyway. It is a Bohemian quarter, perhaps? A district where the law relaxes a trifle?"

McKann replied grimly that he didn't think the name referred to that kind of liberty.

"So much the better," sighed Kitty. "I am a Californian, you know; that's the only part of America I know very well, and out there, when we called a place Liberty Hill or Liberty Hollow— well, we meant it. You will excuse me if I'm uncommunicative, won't you? I must not talk in this raw air. My throat is sensitive after a long programme." She lay back in her corner and closed her eyes.

When the cab rolled down the incline at East Liberty station, the New York express was whistling in. A porter opened the door. McKann sprang out, gave him a claim check and his Pullman ticket, and told him to get his bag at the check-stand and rush it on that train.

Miss Ayrshire, having gathered up her flowers, put out her hand to take his arm. "Why, it's you!" she exclaimed, as she saw his face in the light. "What a coincidence!" She made no further move to alight, but sat smiling as if she had just seated herself in a drawing-room and were ready for talk and a cup of tea.

McKann caught her arm. "You must hurry, Miss Ayrshire, if you mean to catch that train. It stops here only a moment. Can you run?"

"Can I run!" she laughed. "Try me!"

As they raced through the tunnel and up the inside stairway, McKann admitted that he had never before made a dash with feet so quick and sure stepping out beside him. The white-furred boots chased each other like lambs at play, the gold stockings flashed like the spokes of a bicycle wheel in the sun. They reached the door of Miss Ayrshire's state-room just as the train began to pull out. McKann was ashamed of the way he was panting, for Kitty's breathing was as soft and regular as when she was reclining on the back seat of his taxi. It had somehow run in his head that all these stage women were a poor lot physically—unsound, overfed creatures, like canaries that are kept in a cage and stuffed with song-restorer. He retreated to escape her thanks. "Good night! Pleasant journey! Pleasant dreams!" He gave a friendly nod in Kitty's direction and closed the door behind him.

He was somewhat surprised to find his own bag, his Pullman ticket in the strap, on the seat just outside Kitty's door. But there was nothing strange about it. He had got the last section left on the train, No. 13, next the drawing-room. Every other berth on the train was made up. He was just starting to look for the porter when the door of the state-room opened and Kitty Ayrshire came out. She seated herself carelessly in the front seat beside his bag.

"Please talk to me a little," she said coaxingly. "I'm always wakeful after I sing, and I have to hunt some one to talk to. Céline and I get so tired of each other. We can speak very low, and we shall not disturb any one." She crossed her feet and rested her elbow on his Gladstone. Though she still wore her gold slippers and stockings, she did not, he thanked Heaven, have on her concert gown, but a very demure black velvet one with some sort of pearl trimming about the neck. "Wasn't it funny," she proceeded, "that it happened to be you who picked me up? I wanted a word with you, anyway."

McKann smiled in a way that meant he wasn't being taken in. "Did you? We are not very old acquaintances."

"No, perhaps not. But you disapproved to-night, and I

thought I was singing very well. You are very critical in such matters?"

He had been standing, but now he sat down. "My dear young lady, I am not critical at all. I know nothing about such matters."

"And care less?" she said for him. "Well, then we know where we are, in so far as that is concerned. What did displease you? My gown, perhaps? It may seem a little *outré* here, but it's the sort of thing all the imaginative designers abroad are doing, and somebody has to be a missionary and spread the new idea. You like the English sort of concert gown better?"

"About gowns," said McKann, "I know even less than about music. If I looked uncomfortable, it was probably because I was uncomfortable. The seats were bad and the lights were annoying."

Kitty looked up with solicitude. "I was sorry they sold those seats. I don't like to make people uncomfortable in any way. Did the lights give you a headache? They are very trying. They burn one's eyes out in the end, I believe." She paused and waved the porter away with a smile as he came toward them. Half-clad Pittsburghers were tramping up and down the aisle, casting sidelong glances at McKann and his companion. "How much better they look with all their clothes on," she murmured. Then, turning directly to McKann again: "I saw you were not well seated, but I felt something quite hostile and personal. You were displeased with me. Doubtless many people are, but I so seldom get an opportunity to question them. You would be really generous if you took the trouble to tell me why you were displeased."

She spoke frankly, pleasantly, without a shadow of challenge or hauteur. She did not seem to be angling for compliments. McKann settled himself in his seat. He thought he would try her out. She had come for it, and he would let her have it. He found, however, that it was harder to formulate the grounds of his disapproval than he would have supposed. Now that he sat face to face with her, now that she was leaning against his bag, he had no wish to hurt her.

"I'm a hard-headed business man," he said, evasively, "and I don't much believe in any of you fluffy-ruffles people. I have a sort of natural distrust of them all, the men more than the women."

She looked thoughtful. "Artists, you mean?" drawing her words slowly. "What is your business?"

"Coal."

"I don't feel any natural distrust of business men, and I know ever so many. I don't know any coal-men, but I think I could become very much interested in coal. Am I larger-minded than you?"

McKann laughed. "I don't think you know when you are interested or when you are not. I don't believe you know what it feels like to be really interested. There is so much fake about your job. It's an affectation on both sides. I know a great many of the people who went to hear you to-night, and I know that most of them neither know nor care anything about music. They imagine they do because it's supposed to be a fine thing."

Kitty sat upright and looked interested. She was certainly a lovely creature—the only one of her tribe he had ever seen that he would cross the street to see again. Those were remarkable eyes she had—curious, penetrating, restless, somewhat impudent, but not at all dulled by self-conceit. Just now they were rather fierce.

"But isn't that so in everything?" she cried. "How many of your clerks are honest because of a fine, individual sense of honor? They are honest because it is the accepted rule of good conduct in business. Do you know"—she looked at him squarely—"I thought you would have something quite definite to say to me; but this is funny-paper stuff, the sort of objection I'd expect from your office-boy."

"Then you don't think it silly for a lot of people to get together and pretend to enjoy something they know nothing about?"

"Of course I think it silly, but that's the way God made audiences. Don't people go to church in exactly the same way? If there were a spiritual-pressure test-machine at the door to test the congregation I suspect not many of you would get to your pews."

"How do you know I go to church?"

She shrugged her shoulders. "Oh, people with these old, ready-made opinions usually go to church. But you can't evade me like that." She tapped the edge of his seat with the toe of her gold slipper. "You sat there all evening, glaring at me as if you could eat me alive. Now I give you a chance to state your objections, and you merely criticize my audience. What is it? Is it merely that you happen to dislike my personality? In that case, of course, I won't press you."

"No," McKann frowned, "I perhaps dislike your professional personality. As I told you, I have a natural distrust of your variety."

"Natural, I wonder?" Kitty murmured. "I don't see why you should naturally dislike singers any more than I naturally dislike coal-men. I don't classify people by their jobs. Doubtless I should find some coal-men repulsive, and you may find some singers so. But I have reason to believe that, at least, I'm one of the less repelling."

"I don't doubt it," McKann laughed, "and you're a shrewd woman to boot. But you are, all of you, according to my standards, light people. You're brilliant, some of you, but you've no depth."

Kitty seemed to assent, with a dive of her girlish head. "Well, it's a merit in some things to be heavy, and in others to be light. Some things are meant to go deep, and others to go high. Do you want all the women in the world to be profound, or of cast-iron?"

"You are all," he went on steadily, watching her with indulgence, "fed on hectic emotions. You are pampered. You don't help to carry the burdens of the world. You are self-indulgent and appetent."

"Yes, I am," she assented, with a candour which he did not expect. "Not all artists are, but I am. Why not? If I could once get a convincing statement as to why I should not be self-indulgent, I might change my ways. As for the burdens of the world—" Kitty rested her chin on her clasped hands and looked thoughtful. "One should give pleasure to others. My dear sir, granting that the great majority of people can't enjoy anything very keenly, you'll admit that I give pleasure to many more people than you do. One should help others who are less fortunate; at present I am supporting just eighteen people, besides those I hire. There was

never another family in California that had so many crip-
ples and hard-luckers as that into which I had the honor to
be born. The only ones who could take care of themselves
were ruined by the San Francisco earthquake some time
ago. One should make personal sacrifices. I do; I give money
and time and effort to talented students. Oh, I give something much more than that! something that you probably
have never given to any one. I give, to the really gifted ones,
my *wish*, my desire, my light, if I have any; and that, sometimes, when I am tired to death. That, Mr. Worldly Wise-
man, is like giving one's blood! It's the kind of thing you
prudent people never give. That is what was in the box of
precious ointment." Kitty threw off her fervor with a slight
gesture, as if it were a scarf, and leaned back in her seat,
tucking her slipper up on the edge of his. "If you saw the
houses I keep up," she sighed, "and the people I employ, and
the motor-cars I run—And, after all, I've only this to do it
with." She indicated her slender person, which Marshall
could almost have broken in two with his bare hands.

She was, he thought, very much like any other charming
woman, except that she was more so. Her familiarity was
natural and simple. She was at ease because she was not
afraid of him or of herself, or of certain half-clad acquaintances of his who had been wandering up and down the car
oftener than was necessary. Well, he was not afraid, either.

Kitty put her arms over her head and sighed again, feeling the smooth part in her black hair. Her head was small—
capable of great agitation, like a bird's; or of great
resignation, like a nun's. "I can't see why I shouldn't be self-
indulgent, when I indulge others. I can't understand your

equivocal scheme of ethics. Now I can understand Count Tolstoy's, perfectly. I had a long talk with him once, about his book *What is Art?* As nearly as I could get it, he believes that we are a race who can exist only by gratifying appetites; the appetites are evil, and the existence they carry on is evil. We were always sad, he says, without knowing why; even in the stone men. In some miraculous way a divine ideal was disclosed to us, directly at variance with our appetites. It gave us a new craving, which we could only satisfy by starving all the other hungers in us. Happiness lies in ceasing to be and to cause being, because the thing revealed to us is dearer than any existence our appetites can ever get for us. I can understand that. It's something one often feels in art. It is even the subject of the greatest of all operas, which, because I can never hope to sing it, I love more than all the others." Kitty pulled herself up. "Perhaps you agree with Tolstoy?" she added languidly.

"No; I think he's a crank," said McKann, cheerfully.

"What do you mean by a crank?"

"I mean an extremist."

Kitty laughed. "Weighty word! You'll always have a world full of people who keep to the golden mean. Why bother yourself about me and Tolstoy?"

"I don't, except when you bother me."

"Poor man! It's true this isn't your fault. Still, you did provoke it by glaring at me. Why did you go to the concert?"

"I was dragged."

"I might have known!" she chuckled, and shook her head. "No, you don't give me any good reasons. Your morality seems to me the compromise of cowardice, apologetic and sneaking. When righteousness becomes alive and burning, you hate it as much as you do beauty. You want a little of each in your life, perhaps—adulterated, sterilized, with the sting taken out. It's true enough they are both fearsome things when they get loose in the world; they don't, often."

McKann hated tall talk. "My views on women," he said slowly, "are simple."

"Doubtless," Kitty responded, dryly, "but are they consistent? Do you apply them to your stenographers as well as to me? I take it for granted you have unmarried stenographers. Their position, economically, is the same as mine."

McKann studied the toe of her shoe. "With a woman, everything comes back to one thing." His manner was judicial.

She laughed indulgently. "So we are getting down to brass tacks, eh? I have beaten you in argument, and now you are leading trumps." She put her hands behind her head and her lips parted in a half-yawn. "Does everything come back to one thing? I wish I knew. It's more than likely that, under the same conditions, I should have been very like your stenographers—if they are good ones. Whatever I was, I would have been a good one. I think people are a good deal alike. You are more different than any one I have met for some time, but I know that there are a great many more at home like you. And even you—I believe there is a real creature down under these custom-made prejudices that save you the trouble of thinking. If you and I were shipwrecked on a desert island, I have no doubt that we would come to a simple and natural understanding. I'm neither a coward nor a shirk. You would find, if you had to undertake any enterprise of danger or difficulty with a woman, that there are several qualifications quite as important as the one to which you doubtless refer."

McKann felt nervously for his watch-chain. "Of course," he brought out, "I am not laying down any generalizations—" His brows wrinkled.

"Oh, aren't you?" murmured Kitty. "Then I totally misunderstood. But remember"—holding up a finger—"it is you, not I, who are afraid to pursue this subject further. Now, I'll tell you something." She leaned forward and clasped her slim, white hands about her velvet knee. "I am as much a victim of these ineradicable prejudices as you. Your stenographer seems to you a better sort. Well, she does to me. Just because her life is, presumably, grayer than mine, she seems better. My mind tells me that dullness, and a mediocre order of ability, and poverty are not in themselves admirable things. Yet in my heart I always feel that the saleswomen in shops and the working girls in factories are more meritorious than I. Many of them, with my opportunities, would be more selfish than I. Some of them, with their own opportunities, are more selfish. Yet I make this sentimental genuflection before the nun and the charwoman. Tell me, haven't you any weakness? Isn't there any foolish natural thing that unbends you a trifle and makes you feel gay?"

"I like to go fishing."

"To see how many fish you can catch?"

"No, I like the woods and the weather. I like to play a fish and work hard for him. I like the pussy-willows and the cold; and the sky, whether it's blue or gray—night coming on, everything about it."

He spoke devoutly, and Kitty watched him through half-closed eyes. "And you like to feel that there are light-minded girls like me, who only care about the inside of shops and theaters and hotels, eh? You amuse me, you and your fish! But I mustn't keep you any longer. Haven't I given you every opportunity to state your case against me? I thought you would have more to say for yourself. Do you know, I believe it's not a case you have at all, but a grudge. I believe you are envious; that you'd like to be a tenor, and a perfect lady-killer!" She rose, smiling, and paused with her hand on the door of her state-room. "Anyhow, thank you for a pleasant evening. And, by the way, dream of me to-night, and not of either of those ladies who sat beside you. It does not matter much whom we live with in this world, but it matters a great deal whom we dream of." She noticed his bricky flush. "You are very naïf, after all, but, oh, so cautious! You are naturally afraid of everything new, just as I naturally want to try everything: new people, new religions—new miseries, even. If only there were more new things—If only you were really new! I might learn something. I'm like the Queen of Sheba—I'm not above learning. But you, my friend, would be afraid to try a breakfast food. It isn't gravitation that holds the world in place; it's the lazy, obese cowardice of the people on it. All the same"—taking his hand and smiling encouragingly—"I'm going to haunt you a little. *Adios!*"

When Kitty entered her state-room, Céline, in her dressing-gown, was nodding by the window.

"Mademoiselle found the fat gentleman interesting?" she asked. "It is nearly one."

"Negatively interesting. His kind always say the same thing. If I could find one really intelligent man who held his views, I should adopt them."

"Monsieur did not look like an original," murmured Céline, as she began to take down her lady's hair.

McKann slept heavily, as usual, and the porter had to shake him in the morning. He sat up in his berth, and, after composing his hair with his fingers, began to hunt about for his clothes. As he put up the window-blind some bright object in the little hammock over his bed caught the sunlight and glittered. He stared and picked up a delicately turned gold slipper. "Minx! hussy!" he ejaculated. "All that tall talk——! Probably got it from some man who hangs about; learned it off like a parrot. Did she poke this in here herself last night, or did she send that sneak-faced French-woman? It's outrageous!" He wondered whether he might have been breathing audibly when the intruder thrust her head between his curtains. He was conscious that he did not look a Prince Charming in his sleep. He dressed as fast as he could, and, when he was ready to go to the wash-room, glared at the slipper. If the porter should start to make up his berth in his absence— He caught the slipper, wrapped it in his pajama jacket, and thrust it into his bag. He escaped from the train without seeing his tormentor again.

Later McKann threw the slipper into the waste-basket in his room at the Knickerbocker, but the chambermaid, see-ing that it was new and mateless, thought there must be a mistake, and placed it in his clothes-closet. He found it there when he returned from the theater that evening. Considerably mellowed by food and drink and cheerful company, he took the thing in his hand and decided to keep it as a reminder that absurd things could happen to people of the most clocklike deportment. When he got back to Pittsburgh, he stuck it in a lock-box in his vault, safe from prying clerks.

McKann has been ill for five years now, poor fellow! He still goes to the office, because it is the only place that interests him, but his partners do most of the work, and his clerks find him sadly changed—"morbid," they call his state of mind. He has had the pine-trees in his yard cut down because they remind him of cemeteries. On Sundays or holidays, when the office is empty, and he takes his will or his insurance-policies out of his lock-box, he often puts the tarnished gold slipper on his desk and looks at it. Somehow it suggests life to his tired mind, as his pine-trees suggested death—life and youth. When he drops over some day his executors will be puzzled by the slipper.

As for Kitty Ayrshire, she has played so many jokes, practical and impractical, since then, that she has long ago forgotten the night when she threw away a slipper to be a thorn in the side of a just man.

ON THE DIVIDE

NEAR Rattlesnake Creek, on the side of a little draw stood Canute's shanty. North, east, south, stretched the level Nebraska plain of long rust-red grass that undulated constantly in the wind. To the west the ground was broken and rough, and a narrow strip of timber wound along the turbid, muddy little stream that had scarcely ambition enough to crawl over its black bottom. If it had not been for the few stunted cottonwoods and elms that grew along its banks, Canute would have shot himself years ago. The Norwegians are a timber-loving people, and if there is even a turtle pond with a few plum bushes around it they seem irresistibly drawn toward it.

As to the shanty itself, Canute had built it without aid of any kind, for when he first squatted along the banks of Rattlesnake Creek there was not a human being within twenty miles. It was built of logs split in halves, the chinks stopped with mud and plaster. The roof was covered with earth and was supported by one gigantic beam curved in the shape of a round arch. It was almost impossible that any tree had ever grown in that shape. The Norwegians used to say that Canute had taken the log across his knee and bent it into the shape he wished. There were two rooms, or rather there was one room with a partition made of ash saplings interwoven and bound together like big straw basket work. In one corner there was a cook stove, rusted and broken. In the other a bed made of unplaned planks and poles. It was fully eight feet long, and upon it was a heap of dark bed clothing. There was a chair and a bench of colossal proportions. There was an ordinary kitchen cupboard with a few cracked dirty dishes in it, and beside it on a tall box a tin wash-basin. Under the bed was a pile of pint flasks, some broken, some whole, all empty. On the wood box lay a pair of shoes of almost incredible dimensions. On the wall hung a saddle, a gun, and some ragged clothing, conspicuous among which was a suit of dark cloth, apparently new, with a paper collar carefully wrapped in a red silk handkerchief and pinned to the sleeve. Over the door hung a wolf and a badger skin, and on the door itself a brace of thirty or forty snake skins whose noisy tails rattled ominously every time it opened. The strangest things in the shanty were the wide window-sills. At first glance they looked as though they had been ruthlessly hacked and mutilated with a hatchet, but on closer inspection all the notches and holes in the wood took form and shape. There seemed to be a series of pictures. They were, in a rough way, artistic, but the figures were heavy and labored, as though they had been cut very slowly and with very awkward instruments. There were men plowing with little horned imps sitting on their shoulders and on their horses' heads. There were men praying with a skull hanging over their heads and little demons behind them mocking their attitudes. There were men fighting with big serpents, and skeletons dancing together. All about these pictures were blooming vines and foliage such as never grew in this world, and coiled among the branches of the vines there was always the scaly body of a serpent, and behind every flower there was a serpent's head. It was a veritable Dance of Death by one who had felt its sting. In the wood box lay some boards, and every inch of them was cut up in the same manner. Sometimes the work was very rude and careless, and looked as though the hand of the workman had trembled. It would sometimes have been hard to distinguish the men from their evil geniuses but for one fact, the men were always grave and were either toiling or praying, while the devils were always smiling and dancing. Several of these boards had been split for kindling and it was evident that the artist did not value his work highly.

It was the first day of winter on the Divide. Canute stumbled into his shanty carrying a basket of cobs, and after filling the stove, sat down on a stool and crouched his seven foot frame over the fire, staring drearily out of the window at the wide gray sky. He knew by heart every individual clump of bunch grass in the miles of red shaggy prairie that stretched before his cabin. He knew it in all the deceitful loveliness of its early summer, in all the bitter barrenness of its autumn. He had seen it smitten by all the plagues of Egypt. He had seen it parched by drought, and sogged by rain, beaten by hail, and swept by fire, and in the grasshopper years he had seen it eaten as bare and clean as bones that the vultures have left. After the great fires he had seen it stretch for miles and miles, black and smoking as the floor of hell.

He rose slowly and crossed the room, dragging his big

feet heavily as though they were burdens to him. He looked out of the window into the hog corral and saw the pigs burying themselves in the straw before the shed. The leaden gray clouds were beginning to spill themselves, and the snow-flakes were settling down over the white leprous patches of frozen earth where the hogs had gnawed even the sod away. He shuddered and began to walk, trampling heavily with his ungainly feet. He was the wreck of ten winters on the Divide and he knew what they meant. Men fear the winters of the Divide as a child fears night or as men in the North Seas fear the still dark cold of the polar twilight.

His eyes fell upon his gun, and he took it down from the wall and looked it over. He sat down on the edge of his bed and held the barrel towards his face, letting his forehead rest upon it, and laid his finger on the trigger. He was perfectly calm, there was neither passion nor despair in his face, but the thoughtful look of a man who is considering. Presently he laid down the gun, and reaching into the cupboard, drew out a pint bottle of raw white alcohol. Lifting it to his lips, he drank greedily. He washed his face in the tin basin and combed his rough hair and shaggy blond beard. Then he stood in uncertainty before the suit of dark clothes that hung on the wall. For the fiftieth time he took them in his hands and tried to summon courage to put them on. He took the paper collar that was pinned to the sleeve of the coat and cautiously slipped it under his rough beard, looking with timid expectancy into the cracked, splashed glass that hung over the bench. With a short laugh he threw it down on the bed, and pulling on his old black hat, he went out, striking off across the level.

It was a physical necessity for him to get away from his cabin once in a while. He had been there for ten years, digging and plowing and sowing, and reaping what little the hail and the hot winds and the frosts left him to reap. Insanity and suicide are very common things on the Divide. They come on like an epidemic in the hot wind season. Those scorching dusty winds that blow up over the bluffs from Kansas seem to dry up the blood in men's veins as they do the sap in the corn leaves. Whenever the yellow scorch creeps down over the tender inside leaves about the ear, then the coroners prepare for active duty; for the oil of the country is burned out and it does not take long for the flame to eat up the wick. It causes no great sensation there when a Dane is found swinging to his own windmill tower, and most of the Poles after they have become too careless and discouraged to shave themselves keep their razors to cut their throats with.

It may be that the next generation on the Divide will be very happy, but the present one came too late in life. It is useless for men that have cut hemlocks among the mountains of Sweden for forty years to try to be happy in a country as flat and gray and as naked as the sea. It is not easy for men that have spent their youths fishing in the Northern seas to be content with following a plow, and men that have served in the Austrian army hate hard work and coarse clothing and the loneliness of the plains, and long for marches and excitement and tavern company and pretty barmaids. After a man has passed his fortieth birthday it is not easy for him to change the habits and conditions of his life. Most men bring with them to the Divide only the dregs of the lives that they have squandered in other lands and among other peoples.

Canute Canuteson was as mad as any of them, but his madness did not take the form of suicide or religion but of alcohol. He had always taken liquor when he wanted it, as all Norwegians do, but after his first year of solitary life he settled down to it steadily. He exhausted whisky after a while, and went to alcohol, because its effects were speedier and surer. He was a big man with a terrible amount of re-sistant force, and it took a great deal of alcohol even to move him. After nine years of drinking, the quantities he could take would seem fabulous to an ordinary drinking man. He never let it interfere with his work, he generally drank at night and on Sundays. Every night, as soon as his chores were done, he began to drink. While he was able to sit up he would play on his mouth harp or hack away at his window sills with his jack knife. When the liquor went to his head he would lie down on his bed and stare out of the window until he went to sleep. He drank alone and in soli-tude not for pleasure or good cheer, but to forget the awful loneliness and level of the Divide. Milton made a sad blun-der when he put mountains in hell. Mountains postulate faith and aspiration. All mountain peoples are religious. It was the cities of the plains that, because of their utter lack of spirituality and the mad caprice of their vice, were cursed of God.

Alcohol is perfectly consistent in its effects upon man. Drunkenness is merely an exaggeration. A foolish man drunk becomes maudlin; a bloody man, vicious; a coarse man, vulgar. Canute was none of these, but he was morose and gloomy, and liquor took him through all the hells of Dante. As he lay on his giant's bed all the horrors of this world and every other were laid bare to his chilled senses. He was a man who knew no joy, a man who toiled in silence and bitterness. The skull and the serpent were always before him, the symbols of eternal futileness and of eternal hate.

When the first Norwegians near enough to be called neighbors came, Canute rejoiced, and planned to escape from his bosom vice. But he was not a social man by nature and had not the power of drawing out the social side of other people. His new neighbors rather feared him because of his great strength and size, his silence and his lowering brows. Perhaps, too, they knew that he was mad, mad from the eternal treachery of the plains, which every spring stretch green and rustle with the promises of Eden, showing long grassy lagoons full of clear water and cattle whose hoofs are stained with wild roses. Before autumn the lagoons are dried up, and the ground is burnt dry and hard until it blisters and cracks open.

So instead of becoming a friend and neighbor to the men that settled about him, Canute became a mystery and a terror. They told awful stories of his size and strength and of the alcohol he drank. They said that one night, when he went out to see to his horses just before he went to bed, his steps were unsteady and the rotten planks of the floor gave way and threw him behind the feet of a fiery young stallion. His foot was caught fast in the floor, and the nervous horse began kicking frantically. When Canute felt the blood trickling down into his eyes from a scalp wound in his head, he roused himself from his kingly indifference, and with the quiet stoical courage of a drunken man leaned forward and wound his arms about the horse's hind legs and held them against his breast with crushing embrace. All through the darkness and cold of the night he lay there, matching strength against strength. When little Jim Peterson went over the next morning at four o'clock to go with him to the Blue to cut wood, he found him so, and the horse was on its fore knees, trembling and whinnying with fear. This is the story the Norwegians tell of him, and if it is true it is no wonder that they feared and hated this Holder of the Heels of Horses.

One spring there moved to the next "eighty" a family that made a great change in Canute's life. Ole Yensen was too drunk most of the time to be afraid of any one, and his wife Mary was too garrulous to be afraid of any one who listened to her talk, and Lena, their pretty daughter, was not afraid of man nor devil. So it came about that Canute went over to take his alcohol with Ole oftener than he took it alone. After a while the report spread that he was going to marry Yensen's daughter, and the Norwegian girls began to tease Lena about the great bear she was going to keep house for. No one could quite see how the affair had come about, for Canute's tactics of courtship were somewhat peculiar. He apparently never spoke to her at all: he would sit for hours with Mary chattering on one side of him and Ole drinking on the other and watch Lena at her work. She teased him, and threw flour in his face and put vinegar in his coffee, but he took her rough jokes with silent wonder, never even smiling. He took her to church occasionally, but the most watchful and curious people never saw him speak to her. He would sit staring at her while she giggled and flirted with the other men.

Next spring Mary Lee went to town to work in a steam laundry. She came home every Sunday, and always ran across to Yensens to startle Lena with stories of ten cent theatres, firemen's dances, and all the other esthetic delights of metropolitan life. In a few weeks Lena's head was completely turned, and she gave her father no rest until he let her go to town to seek her fortune at the ironing board. From the time she came home on her first visit she began to treat Canute with contempt. She had bought a plush cloak and kid gloves, had her clothes made by the dressmaker, and assumed airs and graces that made the other women of the neighborhood cordially detest her. She generally brought with her a young man from town who waxed his mustache and wore a red necktie, and she did not even introduce him to Canute.

The neighbors teased Canute a good deal until he knocked one of them down. He gave no sign of suffering from her neglect except that he drank more and avoided the other Norwegians more carefully than ever. He lay around in his den and no one knew what he felt or thought, but little Jim Peterson, who had seen him glowering at Lena in church one Sunday when she was there with the town man, said that he would not give an acre of his wheat for Lena's life or the town chap's either; and Jim's wheat was so wondrously worthless that the statement was an exceedingly strong one.

Canute had bought a new suit of clothes that looked as

nearly like the town man's as possible. They had cost him half a millet crop; for tailors are not accustomed to fitting giants and they charge for it. He had hung those clothes in his shanty two months ago and had never put them on, partly from fear of ridicule, partly from discouragement, and partly because there was something in his own soul that revolted at the littleness of the device.

Lena was at home just at this time. Work was slack in the laundry and Mary had not been well, so Lena stayed at home, glad enough to get an opportunity to torment Canute once more.

She was washing in the side kitchen, singing loudly as she worked. Mary was on her knees, blacking the stove and scolding violently about the young man who was coming out from town that night. The young man had committed the fatal error of laughing at Mary's ceaseless babble and had never been forgiven.

"He is no good, and you will come to a bad end by running with him! I do not see why a daughter of mine should act so. I do not see why the Lord should visit such a punishment upon me as to give me such a daughter. There are plenty of good men you can marry."

Lena tossed her head and answered curtly, "I don't happen to want to marry any man right away, and so long as Dick dresses nice and has plenty of money to spend, there is no harm in my going with him."

"Money to spend? Yes, and that is all he does with it I'll be bound. You think it very fine now, but you will change your tune when you have been married five years and see your children running naked and your cupboard empty.

Did Anne Hermanson come to any good end by marrying a town man?"

"I don't know anything about Anne Hermanson, but I know any of the laundry girls would have Dick quick enough if they could get him."

"Yes, and a nice lot of store clothes huzzies you are too. Now there is Canuteson who has an 'eighty' proved up and fifty head of cattle and—"

"And hair that ain't been cut since he was a baby, and a big dirty beard, and he wears overalls on Sundays, and drinks like a pig. Besides he will keep. I can have all the fun I want, and when I am old and ugly like you he can have me and take care of me. The Lord knows there ain't nobody else going to marry him."

Canute drew his hand back from the latch as though it were red hot. He was not the kind of man to make a good eavesdropper, and he wished he had knocked sooner. He pulled himself together and struck the door like a battering ram. Mary jumped and opened it with a screech.

"God! Canute, how you scared us! I thought it was crazy Lou,—he has been tearing around the neighborhood trying to convert folks. I am afraid as death of him. He ought to be sent off, I think. He is just as liable as not to kill us all, or burn the barn, or poison the dogs. He has been worrying even the poor minister to death, and he laid up with the rheumatism, too! Did you notice that he was too sick to preach last Sunday? But don't stand there in the cold,— come in. Yensen isn't here, but he just went over to Sorenson's for the mail; he won't be gone long. Walk right in the other room and sit down."

Canute followed her, looking steadily in front of him and not noticing Lena as he passed her. But Lena's vanity would not allow him to pass unmolested. She took the wet sheet she was wringing out and cracked him across the face with it, and ran giggling to the other side of the room. The blow stung his cheeks and the soapy water flew in his eyes, and he involuntarily began rubbing them with his hands. Lena giggled with delight at his discomfiture, and the wrath in Canute's face grew blacker than ever. A big man humiliated is vastly more undignified than a little one. He forgot the sting of his face in the bitter consciousness that he had made a fool of himself. He stumbled blindly into the living room, knocking his head against the door jamb because he forgot to stoop. He dropped into a chair behind the stove, thrusting his big feet back helplessly on either side of him.

Ole was a long time in coming, and Canute sat there, still and silent, with his hands clenched on his knees, and the skin of his face seemed to have shriveled up into little wrinkles that trembled when he lowered his brows. His life had been one long lethargy of solitude and alcohol, but now he was awakening, and it was as when the dumb stagnant heat of summer breaks out into thunder.

When Ole came staggering in, heavy with liquor, Canute rose at once.

"Yensen," he said quietly, "I have come to see if you will let me marry your daughter today."

"Today!" gasped Ole.

"Yes, I will not wait until tomorrow. I am tired of living alone."

Ole braced his staggering knees against the bedstead,

and stammered eloquently: "Do you think I will marry my daughter to a drunkard? a man who drinks raw alcohol? a man who sleeps with rattle snakes? Get out of my house or I will kick you out for your impudence." And Ole began looking anxiously for his feet.

Canute answered not a word, but he put on his hat and went out into the kitchen. He went up to Lena and said without looking at her, "Get your things on and come with me!"

The tone of his voice startled her, and she said angrily, dropping the soap, "Are you drunk?"

"If you do not come with me, I will take you,—you had better come," said Canute quietly.

She lifted a sheet to strike him, but he caught her arm roughly and wrenched the sheet from her. He turned to the wall and took down a hood and shawl that hung there, and began wrapping her up. Lena scratched and fought like a wild thing. Ole stood in the door, cursing, and Mary howled and screeched at the top of her voice. As for Canute, he lifted the girl in his arms and went out of the house. She kicked and struggled, but the helpless wailing of Mary and Ole soon died away in the distance, and her face was held down tightly on Canute's shoulder so that she could not see whither he was taking her. She was conscious only of the north wind whistling in her ears, and of rapid steady motion and of a great breast that heaved beneath her in quick, irregular breaths. The harder she struggled the tighter those iron arms that had held the heels of horses crushed about her, until she felt as if they would crush the breath from her, and lay still with fear. Canute was striding across the level fields at a pace at which man never went before, drawing the stinging north wind into his lungs in great gulps. He walked with his eyes half closed and looking straight in front of him, only lowering them when he bent his head to blow away the snowflakes that settled on her hair. So it was that Canute took her to his home, even as his bearded barbarian ancestors took the fair frivolous women of the South in their hairy arms and bore them down to their war ships. For ever and anon the soul becomes weary of the conventions that are not of it, and with a single stroke shatters the civilized lies with which it is unable to cope, and the strong arm reaches out and takes by force what it cannot win by cunning.

When Canute reached his shanty he placed the girl upon a chair, where she sat sobbing. He stayed only a few minutes. He filled the stove with wood and lit the lamp, drank a huge swallow of alcohol and put the bottle in his pocket. He paused a moment, staring heavily at the weeping girl, then he went off and locked the door and disappeared in the gathering gloom of the night.

Wrapped in flannels and soaked with turpentine, the little Norwegian preacher sat reading his Bible, when he heard a thundering knock at his door, and Canute entered, covered with snow and with his beard frozen fast to his coat.

"Come in, Canute, you must be frozen," said the little man, shoving a chair towards his visitor.

Canute remained standing with his hat on and said quietly, "I want you to come over to my house tonight to marry me to Lena Yensen."

"Have you got a license, Canute?"

"No, I don't want a license. I want to be married."

"But I can't marry you without a license, man. It would not be legal."

A dangerous light came in the big Norwegian's eye. "I want you to come over to my house to marry me to Lena Yensen."

"No, I can't, it would kill an ox to go out in a storm like this, and my rheumatism is bad tonight."

"Then if you will not go I must take you," said Canute with a sigh.

He took down the preacher's bearskin coat and bade him put it on while he hitched up his buggy. He went out and closed the door softly after him. Presently he returned and found the frightened minister crouching before the fire with his coat lying beside him. Canute helped him put it on and gently wrapped his head in his big muffler. Then he picked him up and carried him out and placed him in his buggy. As he tucked the buffalo robes around him he said: "Your horse is old, he might flounder or lose his way in this storm. I will lead him."

The minister took the reins feebly in his hands and sat shivering with the cold. Sometimes when there was a lull in the wind, he could see the horse struggling through the snow with the man plodding steadily beside him. Again the blowing snow would hide them from him altogether. He had no idea where they were or what direction they were going. He felt as though he were being whirled away in the heart of the storm, and he said all the prayers he knew. But at last the long four miles were over, and Canute set him down in the snow while he unlocked the door. He saw the bride sitting by the fire with her eyes red and swollen as though she had been weeping. Canute placed a huge chair for him, and said roughly,—

"Warm yourself."

Lena began to cry and moan afresh, begging the minister to take her home. He looked helplessly at Canute. Canute said simply,—

"If you are warm now, you can marry us."

"My daughter, do you take this step of your own free will?" asked the minister in a trembling voice.

"No sir, I don't, and it is disgraceful he should force me into it! I won't marry him."

"Then, Canute, I cannot marry you," said the minister, standing as straight as his rheumatic limbs would let him.

"Are you ready to marry us now, sir?" said Canute, laying one iron hand on his stooped shoulder. The little preacher was a good man, but like most men of weak body he was a coward and had a horror of physical suffering, although he had known so much of it. So with many qualms of conscience he began to repeat the marriage service. Lena sat sullenly in her chair, staring at the fire. Canute stood beside her, listening with his head bent reverently and his hands folded on his breast. When the little man had prayed and said amen, Canute began bundling him up again.

"I will take you home, now," he said as he carried him out and placed him in his buggy, and started off with him through the fury of the storm, floundering among the snow drifts that brought even the giant himself to his knees.

After she was left alone, Lena soon ceased weeping. She

was not of a particularly sensitive temperament, and had little pride beyond that of vanity. After the first bitter anger wore itself out, she felt nothing more than a healthy sense of humiliation and defeat. She had no inclination to run away, for she was married now, and in her eyes that was final and all rebellion was useless. She knew nothing about a license, but she knew that a preacher married folks. She consoled herself by thinking that she had always intended to marry Canute some day, any way.

She grew tired of crying and looking into the fire, so she got up and began to look about her. She had heard queer tales about the inside of Canute's shanty, and her curiosity soon got the better of her rage. One of the first things she noticed was the new black suit of clothes hanging on the wall. She was dull, but it did not take a vain woman long to interpret anything so decidedly flattering, and she was pleased in spite of herself. As she looked through the cupboard, the general air of neglect and discomfort made her pity the man who lived there.

"Poor fellow, no wonder he wants to get married to get somebody to wash up his dishes. Batchin's pretty hard on a man."

It is easy to pity when once one's vanity has been tickled. She looked at the window sill and gave a little shudder and wondered if the man were crazy. Then she sat down again and sat a long time wondering what her Dick and Ole would do.

"It is queer Dick didn't come right over after me. He surely came, for he would have left town before the storm began and he might just as well come right on as go back.

If he'd hurried he would have gotten here before the preacher came. I suppose he was afraid to come, for he knew Canuteson could pound him to jelly, the coward!" Her eyes flashed angrily.

The weary hours wore on and Lena began to grow horribly lonesome. It was an uncanny night and this was an uncanny place to be in. She could hear the coyotes howling hungrily a little way from the cabin, and more terrible still were all the unknown noises of the storm. She remembered the tales they told of the big log overhead and she was afraid of those snaky things on the window sills. She remembered the man who had been killed in the draw, and she wondered what she would do if she saw crazy Lou's white face glaring into the window. The rattling of the door became unbearable, she thought the latch must be loose and took the lamp to look at it. Then for the first time she saw the ugly brown snake skins whose death rattle sounded every time the wind jarred the door.

"Canute, Canute!" she screamed in terror.

Outside the door she heard a heavy sound as of a big dog getting up and shaking himself. The door opened and Canute stood before her, white as a snow drift.

"What is it?" he asked kindly.

"I am cold," she faltered.

He went out and got an armful of wood and a basket of cobs and filled the stove. Then he went out and lay in the snow before the door. Presently he heard her calling again.

"What is it?" he said, sitting up.

"I'm so lonesome, I'm afraid to stay in here all alone."

"I will go over and get your mother." And he got up.

"She won't come."

"I'll bring her," said Canute grimly.

"No, no. I don't want her, she will scold all the time."

"Well, I will bring your father."

She spoke again and it seemed as though her mouth was close up to the key-hole. She spoke lower than he had ever heard her speak before, so low that he had to put his ear up to the lock to hear her.

"I don't want him either, Canute,—I'd rather have you."

For a moment she heard no noise at all, then something like a groan. With a cry of fear she opened the door, and saw Canute stretched in the snow at her feet, his face in his hands, sobbing on the door step.

FLAVIA AND HER ARTISTS

✺ ✺

AS the train neared Tarrytown, Imogen Willard began to wonder why she had consented to be one of Flavia's house party at all. She had not felt enthusiastic about it since leaving the city, and was experiencing a prolonged ebb of purpose, a current of chilling indecision, under which she vainly sought for the motive which had induced her to accept Flavia's invitation.

Perhaps it was a vague curiosity to see Flavia's husband, who had been the magician of her childhood and the hero of innumerable Arabian fairy tales. Perhaps it was a desire to see M. Roux, whom Flavia had announced as the especial attraction of the occasion. Perhaps it was a wish to study that remarkable woman in her own setting.

Imogen admitted a mild curiosity concerning Flavia. She was in the habit of taking people rather seriously, but somehow found it impossible to take Flavia so, because of the very vehemence and insistence with which Flavia demanded it. Submerged in her studies, Imogen had, of late years, seen very little of Flavia; but Flavia, in her hurried visits to New York, between her excursions from studio to studio—her luncheons with this lady who had to play at a matinée, and her dinners with that singer who had an evening concert—had seen enough of her friend's handsome daughter to conceive for her an inclination of such violence and assurance as only Flavia could afford. The fact that Imogen had shown rather marked capacity in certain esoteric lines of scholarship, and had decided to specialize in a well-sounding branch of philology at the Ecole des Chartes, had fairly placed her in that category of "interesting people" whom Flavia considered her natural affinities, and lawful prey.

When Imogen stepped upon the station platform she was immediately appropriated by her hostess, whose commanding figure and assurance of attire she had recognized from a distance. She was hurried into a high tilbury and Flavia, taking the driver's cushion beside her, gathered up the reins with an experienced hand.

"My dear girl," she remarked, as she turned the horses up the street, "I was afraid the train might be late. M. Roux insisted upon coming up by boat and did not arrive until after seven."

"To think of M. Roux's being in this part of the world at all, and subject to the vicissitudes of river boats! Why in the world did he come over?" queried Imogen with lively interest. "He is the sort of man who must dissolve and become a shadow outside of Paris."

"Oh, we have a houseful of the most interesting people," said Flavia, professionally. "We have actually managed to get Ivan Schemetzkin. He was ill in California at the close of his concert tour, you know, and he is recuperating with us, after his wearing journey from the coast. Then there is Jules Martel, the painter; Signor Donati, the tenor; Professor Schotte, who has dug up Assyria, you know; Restzhoff, the Russian chemist; Alcée Buisson, the philologist; Frank Wellington, the novelist; and Will Maidenwood, the editor of *Woman*. Then there is my second cousin, Jemima Broadwood, who made such a hit in Pinero's comedy last winter, and Frau Lichtenfeld. *Have* you read her?"

Imogen confessed her utter ignorance of Frau Lichtenfeld, and Flavia went on.

"Well, she is a most remarkable person; one of those advanced German women, a militant iconoclast, and this drive will not be long enough to permit of my telling you her history. Such a story! Her novels were the talk of all Germany when I was there last, and several of them have been suppressed—an honour in Germany, I understand. 'At Whose Door' has been translated. I am so unfortunate as not to read German."

"I'm all excitement at the prospect of meeting Miss Broadwood," said Imogen. "I've seen her in nearly everything she does. Her stage personality is delightful. She always reminds me of a nice, clean, pink-and-white boy who has just had his cold bath, and come down all aglow for a run before breakfast."

"Yes, but isn't it unfortunate that she will limit herself to those minor comedy parts that are so little appreciated in this country? One ought to be satisfied with nothing less than the best, ought one?" The peculiar, breathy tone in which Flavia always uttered that word "best," the most worn in her vocabulary, always jarred on Imogen and always made her obdurate.

"I don't at all agree with you," she said reservedly. "I thought everyone admitted that the most remarkable thing about Miss Broadwood is her admirable sense of fitness, which is rare enough in her profession."

Flavia could not endure being contradicted; she always seemed to regard it in the light of a defeat, and usually colored unbecomingly. Now she changed the subject.

"Look, my dear," she cried, "there is Frau Lichtenfeld now, coming to meet us. Doesn't she look as if she had just escaped out of Walhalla? She is actually over six feet."

Imogen saw a woman of immense stature, in a very short skirt and a broad, flapping sun hat, striding down the hillside at a long, swinging gait. The refugee from Walhalla approached, panting. Her heavy, Teutonic features were scarlet from the rigour of her exercise, and her hair, under her flapping sun hat, was tightly befrizzled about her brow. She fixed her sharp little eyes upon Imogen and extended both her hands.

"So this is the little friend?" she cried, in a rolling baritone.

Imogen was quite as tall as her hostess; but everything, she reflected, is comparative. After the introduction Flavia apologized.

"I wish I could ask you to drive up with us, Frau Lichten-feld."

"Ah, no!" cried the giantess, drooping her head in humorous caricature of a time-honoured pose of the heroines of sentimental romances. "It has never been my fate to be fitted into corners. I have never known the sweet privileges of the tiny."

Laughing, Flavia started the ponies, and the colossal woman, standing in the middle of the dusty road, took off her wide hat and waved them a farewell which, in scope of gesture, recalled the salute of a plumed cavalier.

When they arrived at the house, Imogen looked about her with keen curiosity, for this was veritably the work of Flavia's hands, the materialization of hopes long deferred. They passed directly into a large, square hall with a gallery on three sides, studio fashion. This opened at one end into a Dutch breakfast-room, beyond which was the large dining-room. At the other end of the hall was the music-room. There was a smoking-room, which one entered through the library behind the staircase. On the second floor there was the same general arrangement; a square hall, and, opening from it, the guest chambers, or, as Miss Broadwood termed them, the "cages."

When Imogen went to her room, the guests had begun to return from their various afternoon excursions. Boys were gliding through the halls with ice-water, covered trays, and flowers, colliding with maids and valets who carried shoes and other articles of wearing apparel. Yet, all this was done in response to inaudible bells, on felt soles, and in hushed voices, so that there was very little confusion about it.

Flavia had at last builded her house and hewn out her seven pillars; there could be no doubt, now, that the asylum for talent, the sanatorium of the arts, so long projected, was an accomplished fact. Her ambition had long ago outgrown the dimensions of her house on Prairie Avenue; besides, she had bitterly complained that in Chicago traditions were against her. Her project had been delayed by Arthur's doggedly standing out for the Michigan woods, but Flavia knew well enough that certain of the *aves rares*—"the best"—could not be lured so far away from the seaport, so she declared herself for the historic Hudson and knew no retreat. The establishing of a New York office had at length overthrown Arthur's last valid objection to quitting the lake country for three months of the year; and Arthur could be wearied into anything, as those who knew him knew.

Flavia's house was the mirror of her exultation; it was a temple to the gods of Victory, a sort of triumphal arch. In her earlier days she had swallowed experiences that would have unmanned one of less torrential enthusiasm or blind pertinacity. But, of late years, her determination had told; she saw less and less of those mysterious persons with mysterious obstacles in their path and mysterious grievances against the world, who had once frequented her house on Prairie Avenue. In the stead of this multitude of the unarrived, she had now the few, the select, "the best." Of all that band of indigent retainers who had once fed at her board like the suitors in the halls of Penelope, only Alcée Buisson still retained his right of entrée. He alone had remembered that ambition hath a knapsack at his back, wherein he puts alms to oblivion, and he alone had been considerate enough to do what Flavia had expected of him, and give his name a current value in the world. Then, as Miss Broadwood put it, "he was her first real one,"—and Flavia, like Mahomet, could remember her first believer.

The "House of Song," as Miss Broadwood had called it, was the outcome of Flavia's more exalted strategies. A woman who made less a point of sympathizing with their delicate organisms, might have sought to plunge these phosphorescent pieces into the tepid bath of domestic life; but Flavia's discernment was deeper. This must be a refuge where the shrinking soul, the sensitive brain, should be unconstrained; where the caprice of fancy should outweigh the civil code, if necessary. She considered that this much Arthur owed her; for she, in her turn, had made concessions. Flavia, had, indeed, quite an equipment of epigrams to the effect that our century creates the iron genii which evolve its fairy tales: but the fact that her husband's name was annually painted upon some ten thousand threshing machines, in reality contributed very little to her happiness.

Arthur Hamilton was born, and had spent his boyhood in the West Indies, and physically he had never lost the brand of the tropics. His father, after inventing the machine which bore his name, had returned to the States to patent and manufacture it. After leaving college, Arthur had spent five years ranching in the West and travelling abroad. Upon his father's death he had returned to Chicago and, to the astonishment of all his friends, had taken up the business,—without any demonstration of enthusiasm, but with quiet perseverance, marked ability, and amazing industry. Why or how a self-sufficient, rather ascetic man of thirty, indifferent in manner, wholly negative in all other personal relations, should have doggedly wooed and finally married Flavia Malcolm, was a problem that had vexed older heads than Imogen's.

While Imogen was dressing she heard a knock at her door, and a young woman entered whom she at once recognized as Jemima Broadwood—"Jimmy" Broadwood, she was called by people in her own profession. While there was something unmistakably professional in her frank *savoir-faire*, "Jimmy's" was one of those faces to which the rouge never seems to stick. Her eyes were keen and grey as a windy April sky, and so far from having been seared by calcium lights, you might have fancied they had never looked on anything less bucolic than growing fields and country fairs. She wore her thick, brown hair short and parted at the side; and, rather than hinting at freakishness, this seemed admirably in keeping with her fresh, boyish countenance. She extended to Imogen a large, well-shaped hand which it was a pleasure to clasp.

"Ah! you are Miss Willard, and I see I need not introduce myself. Flavia said you were kind enough to express a wish to meet me, and I preferred to meet you alone. Do you mind if I smoke?"

"Why, certainly not," said Imogen, somewhat disconcerted and looking hurriedly about for matches.

"There, be calm, I'm always prepared," said Miss Broadwood, checking Imogen's flurry with a soothing gesture, and producing an oddly-fashioned silver match-case from some mysterious recess in her dinner-gown. She sat down in a deep chair, crossed her patent-leather Oxfords, and lit her cigarette. "This match-box," she went on meditatively, "once belonged to a Prussian officer. He shot himself in his bath-tub, and I bought it at the sale of his effects."

Imogen had not yet found any suitable reply to make to this rather irrelevant confidence, when Miss Broadwood turned to her cordially: "I'm awfully glad you've come, Miss Willard, though I've not quite decided why you did it.

I wanted very much to meet you. Flavia gave me your thesis to read."

"Why, how funny!" ejaculated Imogen.

"On the contrary," remarked Miss Broadwood. "I thought it decidedly lacked humour."

"I meant," stammered Imogen, beginning to feel very much like Alice in Wonderland, "I meant that I thought it rather strange Mrs. Hamilton should fancy you would be interested."

Miss Broadwood laughed heartily. "Now, don't let my rudeness frighten you. Really, I found it very interesting, and no end impressive. You see, most people in my profession are good for absolutely nothing else, and, therefore, they have a deep and abiding conviction that in some other line they might have shone. Strange to say, scholarship is the object of our envious and particular admiration. Anything in type impresses us greatly; that's why so many of us marry authors or newspapermen and lead miserable lives." Miss Broadwood saw that she had rather disconcerted Imogen, and blithely tacked in another direction. "You see," she went on, tossing aside her half-consumed cigarette, "some years ago Flavia would not have deemed me worthy to open the pages of your thesis—nor to be one of her house party of the chosen, for that matter. I've Pinero to thank for both pleasures. It all depends on the class of business I'm playing whether I'm in favour or not. Flavia is my second cousin, you know, so I can say whatever disagreeable things I choose with perfect good grace. I'm quite desperate for some one to laugh with, so I'm going to fasten myself upon you—for, of course, one can't expect any of these gypsy-dago people to see anything funny. I don't intend you shall lose the humour of the situation. What do you think of Flavia's infirmary for the arts, anyway?"

"Well, it's rather too soon for me to have any opinion at all," said Imogen, as she again turned to her dressing. "So far, you are the only one of the artists I've met."

"One of them?" echoed Miss Broadwood. "One of the *artists*? My offence may be rank, my dear, but I really don't deserve that. Come, now, whatever badges of my tribe I may bear upon me, just let me divest you of any notion that I take myself seriously."

Imogen turned from the mirror in blank astonishment, and sat down on the arm of a chair, facing her visitor. "I can't fathom you at all, Miss Broadwood," she said frankly. "Why shouldn't you take yourself seriously? What's the use of beating about the bush? Surely you know that you are one of the few players on this side of the water who have at all the spirit of natural or ingenuous comedy?"

"Thank you, my dear. Now we are quite even about the thesis, aren't we? Oh! did you mean it? Well, you *are* a clever girl. But you see it doesn't do to permit oneself to look at it in that light. If we do, we always go to pieces, and waste our substance a-starring as the unhappy daughter of the Capulets. But there, I hear Flavia coming to take you down; and just remember I'm not one of them; the artists, I mean."

Flavia conducted Imogen and Miss Broadwood downstairs. As they reached the lower hall they heard voices from the music-room, and dim figures were lurking in the shadows under the gallery, but their hostess led straight to the smoking-room. The June evening was chilly, and a fire had been lighted in the fireplace. Through the deepening dusk the firelight flickered upon the pipes and curious weapons on the wall, and threw an orange glow over the Turkish hangings. One side of the smoking-room was entirely of glass, separating it from the conservatory, which was flooded with white light from the electric bulbs. There was about the darkened room some suggestion of certain chambers in the Arabian Nights, opening on a court of palms. Perhaps it was partially this memory-evoking suggestion that caused Imogen to start so violently when she saw dimly, in a blur of shadow, the figure of a man, who sat smoking in a low, deep chair before the fire. He was long, and thin, and brown. His long, nerveless hands drooped from the arms of his chair. A brown mustache shaded his mouth, and his eyes were sleepy and apathetic. When Imogen entered, he rose indolently and gave her his hand, his manner barely courteous.

"I am glad you arrived promptly, Miss Willard," he said with an indifferent drawl. "Flavia was afraid you might be late. You had a pleasant ride up, I hope?"

"O, very, thank you, Mr. Hamilton," she replied, feeling that he did not particularly care whether she replied at all.

Flavia explained that she had not yet had time to dress for dinner, as she had been attending to Mr. Will Maidenwood, who had become faint after hurting his finger in an obdurate window, and immediately excused herself. As she left, Hamilton turned to Miss Broadwood with a rather spiritless smile.

"Well, Jimmy," he remarked, "I brought up a piano box

full of fireworks for the boys. How do you suppose we'll manage to keep them until the Fourth?"

"We can't, unless we steel ourselves to deny there are any on the premises," said Miss Broadwood, seating herself on a low stool by Hamilton's chair, and leaning back against the mantel. "Have you seen Helen, and has she told you the tragedy of the tooth?"

"She met me at the station, with her tooth wrapped up in tissue paper. I had tea with her an hour ago. Better sit down, Miss Willard;" he rose and pushed a chair toward Imogen, who was standing peering into the conservatory. "We are scheduled to dine at seven, but they seldom get around before eight."

By this time Imogen had made out that here the plural pronoun, third person, always referred to the artists. As Hamilton's manner did not spur one to cordial intercourse, and as his attention seemed directed to Miss Broadwood, in so far as it could be said to be directed to any one, she sat down facing the conservatory and watched him, unable to decide in how far he was identical with the man who had first met Flavia Malcolm in her mother's house, twelve years ago. Did he at all remember having known her as a little girl, and why did his indifference hurt her so, after all these years? Had some remnant of her childish affection for him gone on living, somewhere down in the sealed caves of her consciousness, and had she really expected to find it possible to be fond of him again? Suddenly she saw a light in the man's sleepy eyes, an unmistakable expression of interest and pleasure that fairly startled her. She turned quickly in the direction of his glance, and saw Flavia, just entering, dressed for dinner and lit by the effulgence of her most radiant manner. Most people considered Flavia handsome, and there was no gainsaying that she carried her five-and-thirty years splendidly. Her figure had never grown matronly, and her face was of the sort that does not show wear. Its blond tints were as fresh and enduring as enamel,—and quite as hard. Its usual expression was one of tense, often strained, animation, which compressed her lips nervously. A perfect scream of animation, Miss Broadwood had called it—created and maintained by sheer, indomitable force of will. Flavia's appearance on any scene whatever made a ripple, caused a certain agitation and recognition, and, among impressionable people, a certain uneasiness. For all her sparkling assurance of manner, Flavia was certainly always ill at ease, and even more certainly anxious. She seemed not convinced of the established order of material things, seemed always trying to conceal her feeling that walls might crumble, chasms open, or the fabric of her life fly to the winds in irretrievable entanglement. At least this was the impression Imogen got from that note in Flavia which was so manifestly false.

Hamilton's keen, quick, satisfied glance at his wife had recalled to Imogen all her inventory of speculations about them. She looked at him with compassionate surprise. As a child she had never permitted herself to believe that Hamilton cared at all for the woman who had taken him away from her; and since she had begun to think about them again, it had never occurred to her that any one could become attached to Flavia in that deeply personal and exculsive sense. It seemed quite as irrational as trying to possess oneself of Broadway at noon.

When they went out to dinner, Imogen realized the completeness of Flavia's triumph. They were people of one name, mostly, like kings; people whose names stirred the imagination like a romance or a melody. With the notable exception of M. Roux, Imogen had seen most of them before, either in concert halls or lecture rooms; but they looked noticeably older and dimmer than she remembered them.

Opposite her sat Schemetzkin, the Russian pianist, a short, corpulent man, with an apoplectic face and purplish skin, his thick, iron-grey hair tossed back from his forehead. Next the German giantess sat the Italian tenor—the tiniest of men—pale, with soft, light hair, much in disorder, very red lips and fingers yellowed by cigarettes. Frau Lichtenfeld shone in a gown of emerald green, fitting so closely as to enhance her natural floridness. However, to do the good lady justice, let her attire be never so modest, it gave an effect of barbaric splendour. At her left sat Herr Schotte, the Assyriologist, whose features were effectually concealed by the convergence of his hair and beard, and whose glasses were continually falling into his plate. This gentleman had removed more tons of earth in the course of his explorations than had any of his confrères, and his vigorous attack upon his food seemed to suggest the strenuous nature of his accustomed toil. His eyes were small and deeply set, and his forehead bulged fiercely above his eyes in a bony ridge. His heavy brows completed the leonine suggestion of his face. Even to Imogen, who knew something of his work and greatly respected it, he was entirely too reminiscent of the stone age to be altogether an agreeable dinner companion. He seemed, indeed, to have absorbed something of the savagery of those early types of life which he continually studied.

Frank Wellington, the young Kansas man who had been two years out of Harvard and had published three historical novels, sat next Mr. Will Maidenwood, who was still pale from his recent sufferings, and carried his hand bandaged. They took little part in the general conversation, but, like the lion and the unicorn, were always at it; discussing, every time they met, whether there were or were not passages in Mr. Wellington's works which should be eliminated, out of consideration for the Young Person. Wellington had fallen into the hands of a great American syndicate which most effectually befriended struggling authors whose struggles were in the right direction, and which had guaranteed to make him famous before he was thirty. Feeling the security of his position, he stoutly defended those passages which jarred upon the sensitive nerves of the young editor of *Woman*. Maidenwood, in the smoothest of voices, urged the necessity of the author's recognizing certain restrictions at the outset, and Miss Broadwood, who joined the argument quite without invitation or encouragement, seconded him with pointed and malicious remarks which caused the young editor manifest discomfort. Restzhoff, the chemist, demanded the attention of the entire company for his exposition of his devices for manufacturing ice-cream from vegetable oils, and for administering drugs in bonbons.

Flavia, always noticeably restless at dinner, was somewhat apathetic toward the advocate of peptonized chocolate, and was plainly concerned about the sudden departure of M. Roux, who had announced that it would be necessary for him to leave to-morrow. M. Emile Roux, who sat at Flavia's right, was a man in middle life and quite bald, clearly without personal vanity, though his publishers preferred to circulate only those of his portraits taken in his ambrosial youth. Imogen was considerably shocked at his unlikeness to the slender, black-stocked Rolla he had looked at twenty. He had declined into the florid, settled heaviness of indifference and approaching age. There was, however, a certain look of durability and solidity about him; the look of a man who has earned the right to be fat and bald, and even silent at dinner if he chooses.

Throughout the discussion between Wellington and Will Maidenwood, though they invited his participation, he remained silent, betraying no sign either of interest or contempt. Since his arrival he had directed most of his conversation to Hamilton, who had never read one of his twelve great novels. This perplexed and troubled Flavia. On the night of his arrival, Jules Martel had enthusiastically declared, "There are schools and schools, manners and manners; but Roux is Roux, and Paris sets its watches by his clock." Flavia had already repeated this remark to Imogen. It haunted her, and each time she quoted it she was impressed anew.

Flavia shifted the conversation uneasily, evidently exasperated and excited by her repeated failures to draw the novelist out. "Monsieur Roux," she began abruptly, with her most animated smile, "I remember so well a statement I read some years ago in your 'Mes Etudes des Femmes,' to the effect that you had never met a really intellectual woman. May I ask, without being impertinent, whether that assertion still represents your experience?"

"I meant, madam," said the novelist conservatively, "intellectual in a sense very special, as we say of men in whom the purely intellectual functions seem almost independent."

"And you still think a woman so constituted a mythical personage?" persisted Flavia, nodding her head encouragingly.

"*Une Méduse*, madam, who, if she were discovered, would transmute us all into stone," said the novelist, bowing gravely. "If she existed at all," he added deliberately, "it was my business to find her, and she has cost me many a vain pilgrimage. Like Rudel of Tripoli, I have crossed seas and penetrated deserts to seek her out. I have, indeed, encountered women of learning whose industry I have been compelled to respect; many who have possessed beauty and charm and perplexing cleverness; a few with remarkable information, and a sort of fatal facility."

"And Mrs. Browning, George Eliot, and your own Mme. Dudevant?" queried Flavia with that fervid enthusiasm with which she could, on occasion, utter things simply incomprehensible for their banality—at her feats of this sort Miss Broadwood was wont to sit breathless with admiration.

"Madam, while the intellect was undeniably present in the performances of those women, it was only the stick of the rocket. Although this woman has eluded me, I have studied her conditions and perturbations as astronomers conjecture the orbits of planets they have never seen. If she exists, she is probably neither an artist nor a woman with a mission, but an obscure personage, with imperative intellectual needs, who absorbs rather than produces."

Flavia, still nodding nervously, fixed a strained glance of interrogation upon M. Roux. "Then you think she would be a woman whose first necessity would be to know, whose instincts would be satisfied only with the best, who could draw from others; appreciative, merely?"

The novelist lifted his dull eyes to his interlocutress with an untranslatable smile, and a slight inclination of his shoulders. "Exactly so; you are really remarkable, madam," he added, in a tone of cold astonishment.

After dinner the guests took their coffee in the music-room, where Schemetzkin sat down at the piano to drum rag-time, and give his celebrated imitation of the boarding-school girl's execution of Chopin. He flatly refused to play anything more serious, and would practise only in the morning, when he had the music-room to himself. Hamilton and M. Roux repaired to the smoking-room to discuss the necessity of extending the tax on manufactured articles in France,—one of those conversations which particularly exasperated Flavia.

After Schemetzkin had grimaced and tortured the keyboard with malicious vulgarities for half an hour, Signor Donati, to put an end to his torture, consented to sing, and Flavia and Imogen went to fetch Arthur to play his accompaniments. Hamilton rose with an annoyed look, and placed his cigarette on the mantel. "Why yes, Flavia, I'll accompany him, provided he sings something with a melody, Italian arias or ballads, and provided the recital is not interminable."

"You will join us, M. Roux?"

"Thank you, but I have some letters to write," replied the novelist bowing.

As Flavia had remarked to Imogen, "Arthur really played accompaniments remarkably well." To hear him recalled vividly the days of her childhood, when he always used to spend his business vacations at her mother's home in Maine. He had possessed for her that almost hypnotic influence which young men sometimes exert upon little girls. It was a sort of phantom love affair, subjective and fanciful, a precocity of instinct, like that tender and maternal concern which some little girls feel for their dolls. Yet this childish infatuation is capable of all the depressions and exaltations of love itself; it has its bitter jealousies, cruel disappointments, its exacting caprices.

Summer after summer she had awaited his coming and wept at his departure, indifferent to the gayer young men who had called her their sweetheart, and laughed at everything she said. Although Hamilton never said so, she had been always quite sure that he was fond of her. When he pulled her up the river to hunt for fairy knolls shut about by low, hanging willows, he was often silent for an hour at a time, yet she never felt that he was bored or was neglecting her. He would lie in the sand smoking, his eyes half closed, watching her play and she was always conscious that she was entertaining him. Sometimes he would take a copy of "Alice in Wonderland" in his pocket, and no one could read it as he could, laughing at her with his dark eyes, when anything amused him. No one else could laugh so, with just their eyes, and without moving a muscle of their face. Though he usually smiled at passages that seemed not at all funny to the child, she always laughed gleefully, because he was so seldom moved to mirth that any such demonstration delighted her and she took the credit of it entirely to herself. Her own inclination had been for serious stories, with sad endings, like the Little Mermaid, which he had once told her in an unguarded moment when she had a cold, and was put to bed early on her birthday night and cried because she could not have her party. But he highly disapproved of this preference, and had called it a morbid taste, and always shook his finger at her when she asked for the story. When she had been particularly good, or particularly neglected by other people, then he would sometimes melt and tell her the story, and never laugh at her if she enjoyed the "sad ending" even to tears. When Flavia had taken him away and he came no more, she wept inconsolably for the space of two weeks, and refused to learn her lessons. Then she found the story of the Little Mermaid herself, and forgot him.

Imogen had discovered at dinner that he could still smile at one secretly, out of his eyes, and that he had the old manner of outwardly seeming bored, but letting you know that he was not. She was intensely curious about his exact state of feeling toward his wife, and more curious still to catch a sense of his final adjustment to the conditions of life in general. This, she could not help feeling, she might get again—if she could have him alone for an hour, in some place where there was a little river and a sandy cove bordered by drooping willows, and a blue sky seen through white sycamore boughs.

That evening, before retiring, Flavia entered her husband's room, where he sat in his smoking-jacket, in one of his favourite low chairs.

"I suppose it's a grave responsibility to bring an ardent, serious young thing like Imogen here among all these fascinating personages," she remarked reflectively. "But, after all, one can never tell. These grave, silent girls have their own charm, even for facile people."

"O, so that is your plan?" queried her husband dryly. "I was wondering why you got her up here. She doesn't seem to mix well with the faciles. At least, so it struck me."

Flavia paid no heed to this jeering remark, but repeated, "No, after all, it may not be a bad thing."

"Then do consign her to that shaken reed, the tenor," said her husband yawning. "I remember she used to have a taste for the pathetic."

"And then," remarked Flavia coquettishly, "after all, I owe her mother a return in kind. She was not afraid to trifle with destiny."

But Hamilton was asleep in his chair.

Next morning Imogen found only Miss Broadwood in the breakfast-room.

"Good-morning, my dear girl, whatever are you doing up so early? They never breakfast before eleven. Most of them take their coffee in their room. Take this place by me."

Miss Broadwood looked particularly fresh and encouraging in her blue serge walking-skirt, her open jacket displaying an expanse of stiff, white, shirt bosom, dotted with some almost imperceptible figure, and a dark blue-and-white necktie, neatly knotted under her wide, rolling collar. She wore a white rosebud in the lapel of her coat, and decidedly she seemed more than ever like a nice, clean boy on his holiday. Imogen was just hoping that they would breakfast alone when Miss Broadwood exclaimed, "Ah, there comes Arthur with the children. That's the reward of early rising in this house; you never get to see the youngsters at any other time."

Hamilton entered, followed by two dark, handsome little boys. The girl, who was very tiny, blonde like her mother, and exceedingly frail, he carried in his arms. The boys came up and said good-morning with an ease and cheerfulness uncommon, even in well-bred children, but the little girl hid her face on her father's shoulder.

"She's a shy little lady," he explained, as he put her gently down in her chair. "I'm afraid she's like her father; she can't seem to get used to meeting people. And you, Miss Willard, did you dream of the white rabbit or the little mermaid?"

"O, I dreamed of them all! All the personages of that buried civilization," cried Imogen, delighted that his estranged manner of the night before had entirely vanished, and feeling that, somehow, the old confidential relations had been restored during the night.

"Come, William," said Miss Broadwood, turning to the younger of the two boys, "and what did you dream about?"

"We dreamed," said William gravely—he was the more

assertive of the two and always spoke for both—"we dreamed that there were fireworks hidden in the basement of the carriage-house; lots and lots of fireworks."

His elder brother looked up at him with apprehensive astonishment, while Miss Broadwood hastily put her napkin to her lips, and Hamilton dropped his eyes. "If little boys dream things, they are so apt not to come true," he reflected sadly. This shook even the redoubtable William, and he glanced nervously at his brother. "But do things vanish just because they have been dreamed?" he objected.

"Generally that is the very best reason for their vanishing," said Arthur gravely.

"But, father, people can't help what they dream," remonstrated Edward gently.

"Oh, come! You're making these children talk like a Maeterlinck dialogue," laughed Miss Broadwood.

Flavia presently entered, a book in her hand, and bade them all good-morning. "Come, little people, which story shall it be this morning?" she asked winningly. Greatly excited, the children followed her into the garden. "She does then, sometimes," murmured Imogen as they left the breakfast-room.

"Oh, yes, to be sure," said Miss Broadwood cheerfully. "She reads a story to them every morning in the most picturesque part of the garden. The mother of the Gracchi, you know. She does so long, she says, for the time when they will be intellectual companions for her. What do you say to a walk over the hills?"

As they left the house they met Frau Lichtenfeld and the bushy Herr Schotte—the professor cut an astonishing figure in golf stockings—returning from a walk and engaged in an animated conversation on the tendencies of German fiction.

"Aren't they the most attractive little children," exclaimed Imogen as they wound down the road toward the river.

"Yes, and you must not fail to tell Flavia that you think so. She will look at you in a sort of startled way and say, 'Yes, aren't they?' and maybe she will go off and hunt them up and have tea with them, to fully appreciate them. She is awfully afraid of missing anything good, is Flavia. The way those youngsters manage to conceal their guilty presence in the House of Song is a wonder."

"But don't any of the artist-folk fancy children?" asked Imogen.

"Yes, they just fancy them and no more. The chemist remarked the other day that children are like certain salts which need not be actualized because the formulæ are quite sufficient for practical purposes. I don't see how even Flavia can endure to have that man about."

"I have always been rather curious to know what Arthur thinks of it all," remarked Imogen cautiously.

"Thinks of it!" ejaculated Miss Broadwood. "Why, my dear, what would any man think of having his house turned into an hotel, habited by freaks who discharge his servants, borrow his money, and insult his neighbours? This place is shunned like a lazaretto!"

"Well, then, why does he—why does he—" persisted Imogen.

"Bah!" interrupted Miss Broadwood impatiently, "why did he in the first place? That's the question."

"Marry her, you mean?" said Imogen coloring.

"Exactly so," said Miss Broadwood sharply, as she snapped the lid of her match-box.

"I suppose that is a question rather beyond us, and certainly one which we cannot discuss," said Imogen. "But his toleration on this one point puzzles me, quite apart from other complications."

"Toleration? Why this point, as you call it, simply *is* Flavia. Who could conceive of her without it? I don't know where it's all going to end, I'm sure, and I'm equally sure that, if it were not for Arthur, I shouldn't care," declared Miss Broadwood, drawing her shoulders together.

"But will it end at all, now?"

"Such an absurd state of things can't go on indefinitely. A man isn't going to see his wife make a guy of herself forever, is he? Chaos has already begun in the servants' quarters. There are six different languages spoken there now. You see, it's all on an entirely false basis. Flavia hasn't the slightest notion of what these people are really like, their good and their bad alike escape her. They, on the other hand, can't imagine what she is driving at. Now, Arthur is worse off than either faction; he is not in the fairy story in that he sees these people exactly as they are, *but* he is utterly unable to see Flavia as they see her. There you have the situation. Why can't he see her as we do? My dear, that has kept me awake o' nights. This man who has thought so much and lived so much, who is naturally a critic, really takes Flavia at very nearly her own estimate. But now I am entering upon a wilderness. From a brief acquaintance with her, you can know nothing of the icy fastnesses of Flavia's self-esteem. It's like St. Peter's; you can't realize its magnitude at once. You have to grow into a sense of it by living under its shadow. It has perplexed even Emile Roux, that merciless dissector of egoism. She has puzzled him the more because he saw at a glance what some of them do not perceive at once, and what will be mercifully concealed from Arthur until the trump sounds; namely, that all Flavia's artists have done or ever will do means exactly as much to her as a symphony means to an oyster; that there is no bridge by which the significance of any work of art could be conveyed to her."

"Then, in the name of goodness, why does she bother?" gasped Imogen. "She is pretty, wealthy, well-established; why should she bother?"

"That's what M. Roux has kept asking himself. I can't pretend to analyse it. She reads papers on the Literary Landmarks of Paris, and the Loves of the Poets, and that sort of thing, to clubs out in Chicago. To Flavia it is more necessary to be called clever than to breathe. I would give a good deal to know that glum Frenchman's diagnosis. He has been watching her out of those fishy eyes of his as a biologist watches a hemisphereless frog."

For several days after M. Roux's departure, Flavia gave an embarrassing share of her attention to Imogen. Embarrassing, because Imogen had the feeling of being energetically and futilely explored, she knew not for what. She felt herself under the globe of an air pump, expected to yield up something. When she confined the conversation to matters of general interest, Flavia conveyed to her with some pique that her one endeavour in life had been to fit herself to converse with her friends upon those things which vitally interested them. "One has no right to accept their best from people unless one gives, isn't it so? I want to be able to give—!" she declared vaguely. Yet whenever Imogen strove to pay her tithes and plunged bravely into her plans for study next winter, Flavia grew absent-minded and interrupted her by amazing generalizations or by such embarrassing questions as, "And these grim studies really have charm for you; you are quite buried in them; they make other things seem light and ephemeral?"

"I rather feel as though I had got in here under false pretences," Imogen confided to Miss Broadwood, "I'm sure I don't know what it is that she wants of me."

"Ah," chuckled Jemima, "you are not equal to these heart to heart talks with Flavia. You utterly fail to communicate to her the atmosphere of that untroubled joy in which you dwell. You must remember that she gets no feeling out of things herself, and she demands that you impart yours to her by some process of psychic transmission. I once met a blind girl, blind from birth, who could discuss the peculiarities of the Barbizon school with just Flavia's glibness and enthusiasm. Ordinarily Flavia knows how to get what she wants from people, and her memory is wonderful. One evening I heard her giving Frau Lichtenfeld some random impressions about Hedda Gabler which she extracted from me five years ago; giving them with an impassioned conviction of which I was never guilty. But I have known other people who could appropriate your stories and opinions;

Flavia is infinitely more subtile than that; she can soak up the very thrash and drift of your day dreams, and take the very thrills off your back, as it were."

After some days of unsuccessful effort, Flavia withdrew herself, and Imogen found Hamilton ready to catch her when she was tossed a-field. He seemed only to have been awaiting this crisis, and at once their old intimacy re-established itself as a thing inevitable and beautifully prepared for. She convinced herself that she had not been mistaken in him, despite all the doubts that had come up in later years, and this renewal of faith set more than one question thumping in her brain. "How did he, how can he?" she kept repeating with a tinge of her childish resentment, "what right had he to waste anything so fine?"

When Imogen and Arthur were returning from a walk before luncheon one morning about a week after M. Roux's departure, they noticed an absorbed group before one of the hall windows. Herr Schotte and Restzhoff sat on the window seat with a newspaper between them, while Wellington, Schemetzkin and Will Maidenwood looked over their shoulders. They seemed intensely interested, Herr Schotte occasionally pounding his knees with his fists in ebullitions of barbaric glee. When Imogen entered the hall, however, the men were all sauntering toward the breakfast-room and the paper was lying innocently on the divan. During luncheon the personnel of that window group were unwontedly animated and agreeable,—all save Schemetzkin, whose stare was blanker than ever, as though Roux's mantle of insulting indifference had fallen upon him, in addition to his own oblivious self absorption. Will Maidenwood seemed embarrassed and annoyed; the chemist employed himself with making polite speeches to Hamilton—Flavia did not come down to lunch—and there was a malicious gleam under Herr Schotte's eyebrows. Frank Wellington announced nervously that an imperative letter from his protecting syndicate summoned him to the city.

After luncheon the men went to the golf links, and Imogen, at the first opportunity, possessed herself of the newspaper which had been left on the divan. One of the first things that caught her eye was an article headed "Roux on Tuft Hunters; The Advanced American Woman As He Sees Her; Aggressive, Superficial and Insincere." The entire interview was nothing more nor less than a satiric characterization of Flavia, a-quiver with irritation and vitriolic malice. No one could mistake it; it was done with all his deftness of portraiture. Imogen had not finished the article when she heard a footstep, and clutching the paper she started precipitately toward the stairway as Arthur entered. He put out his hand, looking critically at her distressed face.

"Wait a moment, Miss Willard," he said peremptorily, "I want to see whether we can find what it was that so interested our friends this morning. Give me the paper, please."

Imogen grew quite white as he opened the journal. She reached forward and crumpled it with her hands. "Please don't, please don't," she pleaded, "it's something I don't want you to see. Oh! why will you? It's just something low and despicable that you can't notice."

Arthur had gently loosed her hands and he pointed her to a chair. He lit a cigar and read the article through without comment. When he had finished it, he walked to the fireplace, struck a match, and tossed the flaming journal between the brass andirons.

"You are right," he remarked as he came back, dusting his hands with his handkerchief. "It's quite impossible to comment. There are extremes of blackguardism for which we have no name. The only thing necessary is to see that Flavia gets no wind of this. This seems to be my cue to act; poor girl."

Imogen looked at him tearfully; she could only murmur, "Oh, why did you read it!"

Hamilton laughed spiritlessly. "Come, don't you worry about it. You always took other people's troubles too seriously. When you were little and all the world was gay and everybody happy, you must needs get the Little Mermaid's troubles to grieve over. Come with me into the music-room. You remember the musical setting I once made you for the Lay of the Jabberwock? I was trying it over the other night, long after you were in bed, and I decided it was quite as fine as the Erl-King music. How I wish I could give you some of the cake that Alice ate and make you a little girl again. Then, when you had got through the glass door into the little garden, you could call to me, perhaps, and tell me all the fine things that were going on there. What a pity it is that you ever grew up!" he added, laughing, and Imogen, too, was thinking just that.

At dinner that evening, Flavia, with fatal persistence, insisted upon turning the conversation to M. Roux. She had been reading one of his novels and had remembered anew that Paris set its watches by his clock. Imogen surmised that she was tortured by a feeling that she had not sufficiently appreciated him while she had had him. When she first mentioned his name, she was answered only by the pall of silence that fell over the company. Then everyone began to talk at once, as though to correct a false position. They spoke of him with a fervid, defiant admiration, with the sort of hot praise that covers a double purpose. Imogen fancied she could see that they felt a kind of relief at what the man had done, even those who despised him for doing it; that they felt a spiteful hate against Flavia, as though she had tricked them, and a certain contempt for themselves that they had been beguiled. She was reminded of the fury of the crowd in the fairy tale, when once the child had called out that the king was in his night-clothes. Surely these people knew no more about Flavia than they had known before, but the mere fact that the thing had been said, altered the situation. Flavia, meanwhile, sat chattering amiably, pathetically unconscious of her nakedness.

Hamilton lounged, fingering the stem of his wine glass, gazing down the table at one face after another and studying the various degrees of self-consciousness they exhibited. Imogen's eyes followed his, fearfully. When a lull came in the spasmodic flow of conversation, Arthur, leaning back in his chair, remarked deliberately, "As for M. Roux, his very profession places him in that class of men whom society has never been able to accept unconditionally because it has never been able to assume that they have any ordered notion of taste. He and his ilk remain, with the mountebanks and snake charmers, people indispensable to our civilization, but wholly unreclaimed by it; people whom we receive, but whose invitations we do not accept."

Fortunately for Flavia, this mine was not exploded until just before the coffee was brought. Her laughter was pitiful to hear; it echoed through the silent room as in a vault, while she made some tremulously light remark about her husband's drollery, grim as a jest from the dying. No one responded and she sat nodding her head like a mechanical toy and smiling her white, set smile through her teeth, until Alcée Buisson and Frau Lichtenfeld came to her support.

After dinner the guests retired immediately to their rooms, and Imogen went upstairs on tiptoe, feeling the echo of breakage and the dust of crumbling in the air. She wondered whether Flavia's habitual note of uneasiness were not, in a manner, prophetic, and a sort of unconscious premonition, after all. She sat down to write a letter, but she found herself so nervous, her head so hot and her hands so cold, that she soon abandoned the effort. Just as she was about to seek Miss Broadwood, Flavia entered and embraced her hysterically.

"My dearest girl," she began, "was there ever such an unfortunate and incomprehensible speech made before? Of course it is scarcely necessary to explain to you poor Arthur's lack of tact, and that he meant nothing. But they! Can they be expected to understand? He will feel wretchedly about it when he realizes what he has done, but in the meantime? And M. Roux, of all men! When we were so fortunate as to get him, and he made himself so unreservedly agreeable, and I fancied that, in his way, Arthur quite admired him. My dear, you have no idea what that speech has done. Schemetzkin and Herr Schotte have already sent me word that they must leave us to-morrow. Such a thing from a host!" Flavia paused, choked by tears of vexation and despair.

Imogen was thoroughly disconcerted; this was the first time she had ever seen Flavia betray any personal emotion which was indubitably genuine. She replied with what consolation she could. "Need they take it personally at all? It was a mere observation upon a class of people—"

"Which he knows nothing whatever about, and with whom he has no sympathy," interrupted Flavia. "Ah, my dear, you could not be *expected* to understand. You can't realize, knowing Arthur as you do, his entire lack of any æsthetic sense whatever. He is absolutely *nil*, stone deaf and stark blind, on that side. He doesn't mean to be brutal, it is just the brutality of utter ignorance. They always feel it—they are so sensitive to unsympathetic influences, you know; they know it the moment they come into the house. I have spent my life apologizing for him and struggling to conceal it; but in spite of me, he wounds them; his very attitude, even in silence, offends them. Heavens! do I not know, is it not perpetually and forever wounding me? But there has never been anything so dreadful as this, never! If I could conceive of any possible motive, even!"

"But, surely, Mrs. Hamilton, it was, after all, a mere expression of opinion, such as we are any of us likely to venture upon any subject whatever. It was neither more personal nor more extravagant than many of M. Roux's remarks."

"But, Imogen, certainly M. Roux has the right. It is a part of his art, and that is altogther another matter. Oh, this is not the only instance!" continued Flavia passionately, "I've always had that narrow, bigoted prejudice to contend with. It has always held me back. But this—!"

"I think you mistake his attitude," replied Imogen, feeling a flush that made her ears tingle, "that is, I fancy he is more appreciative than he seems. A man can't be very demonstrative about those things—not if he is a real man. I should not think you would care much about saving the feelings of people who are too narrow to admit of any other point of view than their own." She stopped, finding herself in the impossible position of attempting to explain Hamilton to his wife; a task which, if once begun, would necessitate an entire course of enlightenment which she doubted Flavia's ability to receive, and which she could offer only with very poor grace.

"That's just where it stings most," here Flavia began pacing the floor, "it is just because they have all shown such tolerance, and have treated Arthur with such unfailing consideration, that I can find no reasonable pretext for his rancour. How can he fail to see the value of such friendships on the children's account, if for nothing else! What an advantage for them to grow up among such associations! Even though he cares nothing about these things himself he might realize that. Is there nothing I could say by way of explanation? To them, I mean? If some one were to explain to them how unfortunately limited he is in these things—"

"I'm afraid I cannot advise you," said Imogen decidedly, "but that, at least, seems to me impossible."

Flavia took her hand and glanced at her affectionately, nodding nervously. "Of course, dear girl, I can't ask you to be quite frank with me. Poor child, you are trembling and your hands are icy. Poor Arthur! But you must not judge him by this altogether; think how much he misses in life. What a cruel shock you've had. I'll send you some sherry. Goodnight, my dear."

When Flavia shut the door, Imogen burst into a fit of nervous weeping.

Next morning she awoke after a troubled and restless night. At eight o'clock Miss Broadwood entered in a red and white striped bath-robe.

"Up, up, and see the great doom's image!" she cried, her eyes sparkling with excitement. "The hall is full of trunks, they are packing. What bolt has fallen? It's you, *ma chérie*, you've brought Ulysses home again and the slaughter has begun!" she blew a cloud of smoke triumphantly from her lips and threw herself into a chair beside the bed.

Imogen, rising on her elbow, plunged excitedly into the story of the Roux interview, which Miss Broadwood heard with the keenest interest, frequently interrupting her by exclamations of delight. When Imogen reached the dramatic scene which terminated in the destruction of the newspaper, Miss Broadwood rose and took a turn about the room, violently switching the tasselled cords of her bath-robe.

"Stop a moment," she cried, "you mean to tell me that he had such a heaven-sent means to bring her to her senses and didn't use it, that he held such a weapon and threw it away?"

"Use it?" cried Imogen unsteadily, "of course he didn't! He

bared his back to the tormentor, signed himself over to punishment in that speech he made at dinner, which every one understands but Flavia. She was here for an hour last night and disregarded every limit of taste in her maledictions."

"My dear!" cried Miss Broadwood, catching her hand in inordinate delight at the situation, "do you see what he has done? There'll be no end to it. Why he has sacrificed himself to spare the very vanity that devours him, put rancours in the vessels of his peace, and his eternal jewel given to the common enemy of man, to make them kings, the seed of Banquo kings! He is magnificent!"

"Isn't he always that?" cried Imogen hotly. "He's like a pillar of sanity and law in this house of shams and swollen vanities, where people stalk about with a sort of mad-house dignity, each one fancying himself a king or a pope. If you could have heard that woman talk of him! Why she thinks him stupid, bigoted, blinded by middle-class prejudices. She talked about his having no æsthetic sense, and insisted that her artists had always shown him tolerance. I don't know why it should get on my nerves so, I'm sure, but her stupidity and assurance are enough to drive one to the brink of collapse."

"Yes, as opposed to his singular fineness, they are calculated to do just that," said Miss Broadwood gravely, wisely ignoring Imogen's tears. "But what has been is nothing to what will be. Just wait until Flavia's black swans have flown! You ought not to try to stick it out; that would only make it harder for every one. Suppose you let me telephone your mother to wire you to come home by the evening train?"

"Anything, rather than have her come at me like that

again. It puts me in a perfectly impossible position, and he *is* so fine!"

"Of course it does," said Miss Broadwood sympathetically, "and there is no good to be got from facing it. I will stay, because such things interest me, and Frau Lichtenfeld will stay because she has no money to get away, and Buisson will stay because he feels somewhat responsible. These complications are interesting enough to cold-blooded folk like myself who have an eye for the dramatic element, but they are distracting and demoralizing to young people with any serious purpose in life."

Miss Broadwood's counsel was all the more generous seeing that, for her, the most interesting element of this dénouement would be eliminated by Imogen's departure. "If she goes now, she'll get over it," soliloquized Miss Broadwood, "if she stays she'll be wrung for him, and the hurt may go deep enough to last. I haven't the heart to see her spoiling things for herself." She telephoned Mrs. Willard, and helped Imogen to pack. She even took it upon herself to break the news of Imogen's going to Arthur, who remarked, as he rolled a cigarette in his nerveless fingers:

"Right enough, too. What should she do here with old cynics like you and me, Jimmy? Seeing that she is brim full of dates and formulæ and other positivisms, and is so girt about with illusions that she still casts a shadow in the sun. You've been very tender of her, haven't you? I've watched you. And to think it may all be gone when we see her next. 'The common fate of all things rare,' you know. What a good fellow you are, anyway, Jimmy," he added, putting his hands affectionately on her shoulders.

Arthur went with them to the station. Flavia was so prostrated by the concerted action of her guests that she was able to see Imogen only for a moment in her darkened sleeping chamber, where she kissed her hysterically, without lifting her head, bandaged in aromatic vinegar. On the way to the station both Arthur and Imogen threw the burden of keeping up appearances entirely upon Miss Broadwood, who blithely rose to the occasion. When Hamilton carried Imogen's bag into the car, Miss Broadwood detained her for a moment, whispering as she gave her a large, warm handclasp, "I'll come to see you when I get back to town; and, in the meantime, if you meet any of our artists, tell them you have left Caius Marius among the ruins of Carthage."

THE BOOKKEEPER'S WIFE

$$\maltese \quad \maltese$$

NOBODY but the janitor was stirring about the offices of the Remsen Paper Company, and still Percy Bixby sat at his desk, crouched on his high stool and staring out at the tops of the tall buildings flushed with the winter sunset, at the hundreds of windows, so many rectangles of white electric light, flashing against the broad waves of violet that ebbed across the sky. His ledgers were all in their places, his desk was in order, his office coat on its peg, and yet Percy's smooth, thin face wore the look of anxiety and strain which usually meant that he was behind in his work. He was trying to persuade himself to accept a loan from the company without the company's knowledge. As a matter of fact, he had already accepted it. His books were fixed, the money, in a black-leather bill-book, was already inside his waistcoat pocket.

He had still time to change his mind, to rectify the false figures in his ledger, and to tell Stella Brown that they couldn't possibly get married next month. There he always halted in his reasoning, and went back to the beginning.

The Remsen Paper Company was a very wealthy concern, with easy, old-fashioned working methods. They did a long-time credit business with safe customers, who never thought of paying up very close on their large indebtedness. From the payments on these large accounts Percy had taken a hundred dollars here and two hundred there until he had made up the thousand he needed. So long as he stayed by the books himself and attended to the mail-orders he couldn't possibly be found out. He could move these little shortages about from account to account indefinitely. He could have all the time he needed to pay back the deficit, and more time than he needed.

Although he was so far along in one course of action, his mind still clung resolutely to the other. He did not believe he was going to do it. He was the least of a sharper in the world. Being scrupulously honest even in the most trifling matters was a pleasure to him. He was the sort of young man that Socialists hate more than they hate capitalists. He loved his desk, he loved his books, which had no handwriting in them but his own. He never thought of resenting the fact that he had written away in those books the good red years between twenty-one and twenty-seven. He would have hated to let any one else put so much as a pen-scratch in them. He liked all the boys about the office; his desk, worn smooth by the sleeves of his alpaca coat; his rulers and inks and pens and calendars. He had a great pride in working economics, and he always got so far ahead when supplies were distributed that he had drawers full of pencils and pens and rubber bands against a rainy day.

Percy liked regularity: to get his work done on time, to have his half-day off every Saturday, to go to the theater Saturday night, to buy a new necktie twice a month, to appear in a new straw hat on the right day in May, and to know what was going on in New York. He read the morning and evening papers coming and going on the elevated, and preferred journals of approximate reliability. He got excited about ball-games and elections and business failures, was not above an interest in murders and divorce scandals, and he checked the news off as neatly as he checked his mail-orders. In short, Percy Bixby was like the model pupil who is satisfied with his lessons and his teachers and his holidays, and who would gladly go to school all his life. He had never wanted anything outside his routine until he wanted Stella Brown to marry him, and that had upset everything.

It wasn't, he told himself for the hundredth time, that she was extravagant. Not a bit of it. She was like all girls. Moreover, she made good money, and why should she marry unless she could better herself? The trouble was that he had lied to her about his salary. There were a lot of fellows rushing Mrs. Brown's five daughters, and they all seemed to have fixed on Stella as first choice and this or that one of the sisters as second. Mrs. Brown thought it proper to drop an occasional hint in the presence of these young men to the effect that she expected Stella to "do well." It went without saying that hair and complexion like Stella's could scarcely be expected to do poorly. Most of the boys who went to the house and took the girls out in a bunch to dances and movies seemed to realize this. They merely wanted a whirl with Stella before they settled down to one of her sisters. It was tacitly understood that she came too high for them. Percy had sensed all this through those slumbering instincts which awake in us all to befriend us in love or in danger.

But there was one of his rivals, he knew, who was a man to be reckoned with. Charley Greengay was a young salesman who wore tailor-made clothes and spotted waistcoats, and had a necktie for every day in the month. His air was that of a young man who is out for things that come high and who is going to get them. Mrs. Brown was ever and again dropping a word before Percy about how the girl that took Charley would have her flat furnished by the best furniture people, and her china-closet stocked with the best ware, and would have nothing to worry about but nicks and scratches. It was because he felt himself pitted against this pulling power of Greengay's that Percy had brazenly lied to Mrs. Brown, and told her that his salary had been raised to fifty a week, and that now he wanted to get married.

When he threw out this challenge to Mother Brown, Percy was getting thirty-five dollars a week, and he knew well enough that there were several hundred thousand young men in New York who would do his work as well as he did for thirty.

These were the factors in Percy's present situation. He went over them again and again as he sat stooping on his tall stool. He had quite lost track of time when he heard the janitor call good night to the watchman. Without thinking what he was doing, he slid into his overcoat, caught his hat, and rushed out to the elevator, which was waiting for the janitor. The moment the car dropped, it occurred to him that the thing was decided without his having made up his mind at all. The familiar floors passed him, ten, nine, eight, seven. By the time he reached the fifth, there was no possibility of going back; the click of the drop-lever seemed to settle that. The money was in his pocket. Now, he told himself as he hurried out into the exciting clamor of the street, he was not going to worry about it any more.

———

WHEN Percy reached the Browns' flat on 123d Street that evening he felt just the slightest chill in Stella's greeting. He could make that all right, he told himself, as he kissed her lightly in the dark three-by-four entrance-hall. Percy's courting had been prosecuted mainly in the Bronx or in winged pursuit of a Broadway car. When he entered the crowded sitting-room he greeted Mrs. Brown respectfully and the four girls playfully. They were all piled on one couch, reading the continued story in the evening paper, and they didn't think it necessary to assume more formal attitudes for Percy. They looked up over the smeary pink sheets of paper, and handed him, as Percy said, the same old jolly:

"Hullo, Perc'! Come to see me, ain't you? So flattered!"

"Any sweet goods on you, Perc'? Anything doing in the bong-bong line tonight?"

"Look at his new neckwear! Say, Perc', remember me. That tie would go lovely with my new tailored waist."

"Quit your kiddin', girls!" called Mrs. Brown, who was drying shirt-waists on the dining-room radiator. "And, Percy, mind the rugs when you're steppin' round among them gum-drops."

Percy fired his last shot at the recumbent figures, and followed Stella into the dining-room, where the table and two large easy-chairs formed, in Mrs. Brown's estimation, a proper background for a serious suitor.

"I say, Stell'," he began as he walked about the table with his hands in his pockets, "seems to me we ought to begin buying our stuff." She brightened perceptibly. "Ah," Percy thought, "so that *was* the trouble!" "To-morrow's Saturday; why can't we make an afternoon of it?" he went on cheer-fully. "Shop till we're tired, then go to Houtin's for dinner, and end up at the theater."

As they bent over the lists she had made of things needed, Percy glanced at her face. She was very much out of her sisters' class and out of his, and he kept congratulating himself on his nerve. He was going in for something much too handsome and expensive and distinguished for him, he felt, and it took courage to be a plunger. To begin with, Stella was the sort of girl who had to be well dressed. She had pale primrose hair, with bluish tones in it, very soft and fine, so that it lay smooth however she dressed it, and pale-blue eyes, with blond eyebrows and long, dark lashes. She would have been a little too remote and languid even for the fastidious Percy had it not been for her hard, practical mouth, with lips that always kept their pink even when the rest of her face was pale. Her employers, who at first might be struck by her indifference, understood that anybody with that sort of mouth would get through the work.

After the shopping-lists had been gone over, Percy took up the question of the honeymoon. Stella said she had been thinking of Atlantic City. Percy met her with firmness. Whatever happened, he couldn't leave his books now.

"I want to do my traveling right here on Forty-second

Street, with a high-price show every night," he declared. He made out an itinerary, punctuated by theaters and restaurants, which Stella consented to accept as a substitute for Atlantic City.

"They give your fellows a week off when they're married, don't they?" she asked.

"Yes, but I'll want to drop into the office every morning to look after my mail. That's only businesslike."

"I'd like to have you treated as well as the others, though." Stella turned the rings about on her pale hand and looked at her polished finger-tips.

"I'll look out for that. What do you say to a little walk, Stell'?" Percy put the question coaxingly. When Stella was pleased with him she went to walk with him, since that was the only way in which Percy could ever see her alone. When she was displeased, she said she was too tired to go out. To-night she smiled at him incredulously, and went to put on her hat and gray fur piece.

Once they were outside, Percy turned into a shadowy side street that was only partly built up, a dreary waste of derricks and foundation holes, but comparatively solitary. Stella liked Percy's steady, sympathetic silences; she was not a chatterbox herself. She often wondered why she was going to marry Bixby instead of Charley Greengay. She knew that Charley would go further in the world. Indeed, she had often coolly told herself that Percy would never go very far. But, as she admitted with a shrug, she was "weak to Percy." In the capable New York stenographer, who estimated values coldly and got the most for the least outlay, there was something left that belonged to another kind of woman—

something that liked the very things in Percy that were not good business assets. However much she dwelt upon the effectiveness of Greengay's dash and color and assurance, her mind always came back to Percy's neat little head, his clean-cut face, and warm, clear, gray eyes, and she liked them better than Charley's fullness and blurred floridness. Having reckoned up their respective chances with no doubtful result, she opposed a mild obstinacy to her own good sense. "I guess I'll take Percy, *anyway*," she said simply, and that was all the good her clever business brain did her.

————

PERCY spent a night of torment, lying tense on his bed in the dark, and figuring out how long it would take him to pay back the money he was advancing to himself. Any fool could do it in five years, he reasoned, but he was going to do it in three. The trouble was that his expensive courtship had taken every penny of his salary. With competitors like Charley Greengay, you had to spend money or drop out. Certain birds, he reflected ruefully, are supplied with more attractive plumage when they are courting, but nature hadn't been so thoughtful for men. When Percy reached the office in the morning he climbed on his tall stool and leaned his arms on his ledger. He was so glad to feel it there that he was faint and weak-kneed.

————

OLIVER REMSEN, JUNIOR, had brought new blood into the Remsen Paper Company. He married shortly after Percy Bixby did, and in the five succeeding years he had considerably enlarged the company's business and profits. He had been particularly successful in encouraging efficiency and loyalty in the employees. From the time he came into the office he had stood for shorter hours, longer holidays, and a generous consideration of men's necessities. He came out of college on the wave of economic reform, and he continued to read and think a good deal about how the machinery of labor is operated. He knew more about the men who worked for him than their mere office records.

Young Remsen was troubled about Percy Bixby because he took no summer vacations—always asked for the two weeks' extra pay instead. Other men in the office had skipped a vacation now and then, but Percy had stuck to his desk for five years, had tottered to his stool through attacks of grippe and tonsilitis. He seemed to have grown fast to his ledger, and it was to this that Oliver objected. He liked his men to stay men, to look like men and live like men. He remembered how alert and wide-awake Bixby had seemed to him when he himself first came into the office. He had picked Bixby out as the most intelligent and interested of his father's employees, and since then had often wondered why he never seemed to see chances to forge ahead. Promotions, of course, went to the men who went after them. When Percy's baby died, he went to the funeral, and asked Percy to call on him if he needed money. Once when he chanced to sit down by Bixby on the elevated and found him reading Bryce's "American Commonwealth," he asked him to make use of his own large office library. Percy thanked him, but he never came for any books. Oliver wondered whether his bookkeeper really tried to avoid him.

One evening Oliver met the Bixbys in the lobby of a theater. He introduced Mrs. Remsen to them, and held them for some moments in conversation. When they got into their motor, Mrs. Remsen said:

"Is that little man afraid of you, Oliver? He looked like a scared rabbit."

Oliver snapped the door, and said with a shade of irritation:

"I don't know what's the matter with him. He's the fellow I've told you about who never takes a vacation. I half believe it's his wife. She looks pitiless enough for anything."

"She's very pretty of her kind," mused Mrs. Remsen, "but rather chilling. One can see that she has ideas about elegance."

"Rather unfortunate ones for a bookkeeper's wife. I surmise that Percy felt she was overdressed, and that made him awkward with me. I've always suspected that fellow of good taste."

After that, when Remsen passed the counting-room and saw Percy screwed up over his ledger, he often remembered Mrs. Bixby, with her cold, pale eyes and long lashes, and her expression that was something between indifference and discontent. She rose behind Percy's bent shoulders like an apparition.

One spring afternoon Remsen was closeted in his private office with his lawyer until a late hour. As he came down the long hall in the dusk he glanced through the glass partition into the counting-room, and saw Percy Bixby huddled up on his tall stool, though it was too dark to work. Indeed,

Bixby's ledger was closed, and he sat with his two arms resting on the brown cover. He did not move a muscle when young Remsen entered.

"You are late, Bixby, and so am I," Oliver began genially as he crossed to the front of the room and looked out at the lighted windows of other tall buildings. "The fact is, I've been doing something that men have a foolish way of putting off. I've been making my will."

"Yes, sir." Percy brought it out with a deep breath.

"Glad to be through with it," Oliver went on. "Mr. Melton will bring the paper back to-morrow, and I'd like to ask you to be one of the witnesses."

"I' d be very proud, Mr. Remsen."

"Thank you, Bixby. Good night." Remsen took up his hat just as Percy slid down from his stool.

"Mr. Remsen, I'm told you're going to have the books gone over."

"Why, yes, Bixby. Don't let that trouble you. I 'm taking in a new partner, you know, an old college friend. Just because he is a friend, I insist upon all the usual formalities. But it is a formality, and I'll guarantee the expert won't make a scratch on your books. Good night. You'd better be coming, too." Remsen had reached the door when he heard "Mr. Remsen!" in a desperate voice behind him. He turned, and saw Bixby standing uncertainly at one end of the desk, his hand still on his ledger, his uneven shoulders drooping forward and his head hanging as if he were seasick. Remsen came back and stood at the other end of the long desk. It was too dark to see Bixby's face clearly.

"What is it, Bixby?"

"Mr. Remsen, five years ago, just before I was married, I falsified the books a thousand dollars, and I used the money." Percy leaned forward against his desk, which took him just across the chest.

"What's that, Bixby?" Young Remsen spoke in a tone of polite surprise. He felt painfully embarrassed.

"Yes, sir. I thought I'd get it all paid back before this. I've put back three hundred, but the books are still seven hundred out of true. I've played the shortages about from account to account these five years, but an expert would find 'em in twenty-four hours."

"I don't just understand how—" Oliver stopped and shook his head.

"I held it out of the Western remittances, Mr. Remsen. They were coming in heavy just then. I was up against it. I hadn't saved anything to marry on, and my wife thought I was getting more money than I was. Since we've been married, I've never had the nerve to tell her. I could have paid it all back if it hadn't been for the unforeseen expenses."

Remsen sighed.

"Being married is largely unforeseen expenses, Percy. There's only one way to fix this up: I'll give you seven hundred dollars in cash to-morrow, and you can give me your personal note, with the understanding that I hold ten dollars a week out of your pay-check until it is paid. I think you ought to tell your wife exactly how you are fixed, though. You can't expect her to help you much when she doesn't know."

———

THAT night Mrs. Bixby was sitting in their flat, waiting for her husband. She was dressed for a bridge party, and often looked with impatience from her paper to the Mission clock, as big as a coffin and with nothing but two weights dangling in its hollow framework. Percy had been loath to buy the clock when they got their furniture, and he had hated it ever since. Stella had changed very little since she came into the flat a bride. Then she wore her hair in a Floradora pompadour; now she wore it hooded close about her head like a scarf, in a rather smeary manner, like an Impressionist's brush-work. She heard her husband come in and close the door softly. While he was taking off his hat in the narrow tunnel of a hall, she called to him:

"I hope you've had something to eat down-town. You'll have to dress right away." Percy came in and sat down. She looked up from the evening paper she was reading. "You've no time to sit down. We must start in fifteen minutes."

He shaded his eyes from the glaring overhead light.

"I'm afraid I can't go anywhere to-night. I'm all in."

Mrs. Bixby rattled her paper, and turned from the theatrical page to the fashions.

"You'll feel better after you dress. We won't stay late."

Her even persistence usually conquered her husband. She never forgot anything she had once decided to do. Her manner of following it up grew more chilly, but never weaker. To-night there was no spring in Percy. He closed his eyes and replied without moving:

"I can't go. You had better telephone the Burks we aren't coming. I have to tell you something disagreeable."

Stella rose.

"I certainly am not going to disappoint the Burks and stay at home to talk about anything disagreeable."

"You're not very sympathetic, Stella."

She turned away.

"If I were, you'd soon settle down into a pretty dull proposition. We'd have no social life now if I didn't keep at you."

Percy roused himself a little.

"Social life? Well, we'll have to trim that pretty close for a while. I'm in debt to the company. We've been living beyond our means ever since we were married."

"We can't live on less than we do," Stella said quietly. "No use in taking that up again."

Percy sat up, clutching the arms of his chair.

"We'll have to take it up. I'm seven hundred dollars short, and the books are to be audited to-morrow. I told young Remsen and he's going to take my note and hold the money out of my pay-checks. He could send me to jail, of course."

Stella turned and looked down at him with a gleam of interest.

"Oh, you've been playing solitaire with the books, have you? And he's found you out! I hope I'll never see that man again. Sugar face!" She said this with intense acrimony. Her forehead flushed delicately, and her eyes were full of hate. Young Remsen was not her idea of a "business man."

Stella went into the other room. When she came back she wore her evening coat and carried long gloves and a black scarf. This she began to arrange over her hair before the mirror above the false fireplace. Percy lay inert in the Morris chair and watched her. Yes, he understood; it was very difficult for a woman with hair like that to be shabby and to go without things. Her hair made her conspicuous, and it had to be lived up to. It had been the deciding factor in his fate.

Stella caught the lace over one ear with a large gold hairpin. She repeated this until she got a good effect. Then turning to Percy, she began to draw on her gloves.

"I'm not worrying any, because I'm going back into business," she said firmly. "I meant to, anyway, if you didn't get a raise the first of the year. I have the offer of a good position, and we can live in an apartment hotel."

Percy was on his feet in an instant.

"I won't have you grinding in any office. That's flat."

Stella's lower lip quivered in a commiserating smile. "Oh, I won't lose my health. Charley Greengay's a partner in his concern now, and he wants a private secretary."

Percy drew back.

"You can't work for Greengay. He's got too bad a reputation. You've more pride than that, Stella."

The thin sweep of color he knew so well went over Stella's face.

"His business reputation seems to be all right," she commented, working the kid on with her left hand.

"What if it is?" Percy broke out. "He's the cheapest kind of a skate. He gets into scrapes with the girls in his own office. The last one got into the newspapers, and he had to pay the girl a wad."

"He don't get into scrapes with his books, anyway, and

he seems to be able to stand getting into the papers. I excuse Charley. His wife's a pill."

"I suppose you think he'd have been all right if he'd married you," said Percy, bitterly.

"Yes, I do." Stella buttoned her glove with an air of finishing something, and then looked at Percy without animosity. "Charley and I both have sporty tastes, and we like excitement. You might as well live in Newark if you're going to sit at home in the evening. You oughtn't to have married a business woman; you need somebody domestic. There's nothing in this sort of life for either of us."

"That means, I suppose, that you're going around with Greengay and his crowd?"

"Yes, that's my sort of crowd, and you never did fit into it. You're too intellectual. I've always been proud of you, Percy. You're better style than Charley, but that gets tiresome. You will never burn much red fire in New York, now, will you?"

Percy did not reply. He sat looking at the minute-hand of the eviscerated Mission clock. His wife almost never took the trouble to argue with him.

"You're old style, Percy," she went on. "Of course everybody marries and wishes they hadn't, but nowadays people get over it. Some women go ahead on the quiet, but I'm giving it to you straight. I'm going to work for Greengay. I like his line of business, and I meet people well. Now I'm going to the Burks'."

Percy dropped his hands limply between his knees.

"I suppose," he brought out, "the real trouble is that you've decided my earning power is not very great."

"That's part of it, and part of it is you're old fashioned." Stella paused at the door and looked back. "What made you rush me, anyway, Percy?" she asked indulgently. "What did you go and pretend to be a spender and get tied up with me for?"

"I guess everybody wants to be a spender when he's in love," Percy replied.

Stella shook her head mournfully.

"No, you're a spender or you're not. Greengay has been broke three times, fired, down and out, black-listed. But he's always come back, and he always will. You will never be fired, but you'll always be poor." She turned and looked back again before she went out.

———

SIX months later Bixby came to young Oliver Remsen one afternoon and said he would like to have twenty dollars a week held out of his pay until his debt was cleared off.

Oliver looked up at his sallow employee and asked him how he could spare as much as that.

"My expenses are lighter," Bixby replied. "My wife has gone into business with a ready-to-wear firm. She is not living with me any more."

Oliver looked annoyed, and asked him if nothing could be done to readjust his domestic affairs. Bixby said no; they would probably remain as they were.

"But where are you living, Bixby? How have you arranged things?" the young man asked impatiently.

"I'm very comfortable. I live in a boarding-house and have my own furniture. There are several fellows there who are fixed the same way. Their wives went back into business, and they drifted apart."

With a baffled expression Remsen stared at the uneven shoulders under the skin-fitting alpaca desk coat as his bookkeeper went out. He had meant to do something for Percy, but somehow, he reflected, one never did do anything for a fellow who had been stung as hard as that.

HER BOSS

P AUL WANNING opened the front door of his house
in Orange, closed it softly behind him, and stood looking about the hall as he drew off his gloves.

Nothing was changed there since last night, and yet he
stood gazing about him with an interest which a long-mar-
ried man does not often feel in his own reception hall. The
rugs, the two pillars, the Spanish tapestry chairs, were all
the same. The Venus di Medici stood on her column as
usual and there, at the end of the hall (opposite the front
door), was the full-length portrait of Mrs. Wanning, ma-
turely blooming forth in an evening gown, signed with the
name of a French painter who seemed purposely to have
made his signature indistinct. Though the signature was
largely what one paid for, one couldn't ask him to do it
over.

In the dining room the colored man was moving about
the table set for dinner, under the electric cluster. The candles had not yet been lighted. Wanning watched him with
a homesick feeling in his heart. They had had Sam a long
while, twelve years, now. His warm hall, the lighted dining-
room, the drawing room where only the flicker of the wood
fire played upon the shining surfaces of many objects—
they seemed to Wanning like a haven of refuge. It had never

occurred to him that his house was too full of things. He often said, and he believed, that the women of his household had "perfect taste." He had paid for these objects, sometimes with difficulty, but always with pride. He carried a heavy life-insurance and permitted himself to spend most of the income from a good law practise. He wished, during his life-time, to enjoy the benefits of his wife's discriminating extravagance.

Yesterday Wanning's doctor had sent him to a specialist. Today the specialist, after various laboratory tests, had told him most disconcerting things about the state of very necessary, but hitherto wholly uninteresting, organs of his body.

The information pointed to something incredible; insinuated that his residence in this house was only temporary; that he, whose time was so full, might have to leave not only his house and his office and his club, but a world with which he was extremely well satisfied—the only world he knew anything about.

Wanning unbuttoned his overcoat, but did not take it off. He stood folding his muffler slowly and carefully. What he did not understand was, how he could go while other people stayed. Sam would be moving about the table like this, Mrs. Wanning and her daughters would be dressing upstairs, when he would not be coming home to dinner any more; when he would not, indeed, be dining anywhere.

Sam, coming to turn on the parlor lights, saw Wanning and stepped behind him to take his coat.

"Good evening, Mr. Wanning, sah, excuse me. You entahed so quietly, sah, I didn't heah you."

The master of the house slipped out of his coat and went languidly upstairs.

He tapped at the door of his wife's room, which stood ajar.

"Come in, Paul," she called from her dressing table.

She was seated, in a violet dressing gown, giving the last touches to her coiffure, both arms lifted. They were firm and white, like her neck and shoulders. She was a handsome woman of fifty-five,—still a woman, not an old person, Wanning told himself, as he kissed her cheek. She was heavy in figure, to be sure, but she had kept, on the whole, presentable outlines. Her complexion was good, and she wore less false hair than either of her daughters.

Wanning himself was five years older, but his sandy hair did not show the gray in it, and since his mustache had begun to grow white he kept it clipped so short that it was unobtrusive. His fresh skin made him look younger than he was. Not long ago he had overheard the stenographers in his law office discussing the ages of their employers. They had put him down at fifty, agreeing that his two partners must be considerably older than he—which was not the case. Wanning had an especially kindly feeling for the little new girl, a copyist, who had exclaimed that "Mr. Wanning couldn't be fifty; he seemed so boyish!"

Wanning lingered behind his wife, looking at her in the mirror.

"Well, did you tell the girls, Julia?" he asked, trying to speak casually.

Mrs. Wanning looked up and met his eyes in the glass. "The girls?"

She noticed a strange expression come over his face.

"About your health, you mean? Yes, dear, but I tried not to alarm them. They feel dreadfully. I'm going to have a talk with Dr. Seares myself. These specialists are all alarmists, and I've often heard of his frightening people."

She rose and took her husband's arm, drawing him toward the fireplace.

"You are not going to let this upset you, Paul? If you take care of yourself, everything will come out all right. You have always been so strong. One has only to look at you."

"Did you," Wanning asked, "say anything to Harold?"

"Yes, of course. I saw him in town today, and he agrees with me that Seares draws the worst conclusions possible. He says even the young men are always being told the most terrifying things. Usually they laugh at the doctors and do as they please. You certainly don't look like a sick man, and you don't feel like one, do you?"

She patted his shoulder, smiled at him encouragingly, and rang for the maid to come and hook her dress.

When the maid appeared at the door, Wanning went out through the bath-room to his own sleeping chamber. He was too much dispirited to put on a dinner coat, though such remissness was always noticed. He sat down and waited for the sound of the gong, leaving his door open, on the chance that perhaps one of his daughters would come in.

When Wanning went down to dinner he found his wife already at her chair, and the table laid for four.

"Harold," she explained, "is not coming home. He has to attend a first night in town."

A moment later their two daughters entered, obviously

"dressed." They both wore earrings and masses of hair. The daughters' names were Roma and Florence,—Roma, Firenze, one of the young men who came to the house often, but not often enough, had called them. Tonight they were going to a rehearsal of "The Dances of the Nations,"—a benefit performance in which Miss Roma was to lead the Spanish dances, her sister the Grecian.

The elder daughter had often been told that her name suited her admirably. She looked, indeed, as we are apt to think the unrestrained beauties of later Rome must have looked,—but as their portrait busts emphatically declare they did not. Her head was massive, her lips full and crimson, her eyes large and heavy-lidded, her forehead low. At costume balls and in living pictures she was always Semiramis, or Poppea, or Theodora. Barbaric accessories brought out something cruel and even rather brutal in her handsome face. The men who were attracted to her were somehow afraid of her.

Florence was slender, with a long, graceful neck, a restless head, and a flexible mouth—discontent lurked about the corners of it. Her shoulders were pretty, but her neck and arms were too thin. Roma was always struggling to keep within a certain weight—her chin and upper arms grew persistently more solid—and Florence was always striving to attain a certain weight. Wanning used sometimes to wonder why these disconcerting fluctuations could not go the other way; why Roma could not melt away as easily as did her sister, who had to be sent to Palm Beach to save the precious pounds.

"I don't see why you ever put Rickie Allen in charge of

the English country dances," Florence said to her sister, as they sat down. "He knows the figures, of course, but he has no real style."

Roma looked annoyed. Rickie Allen was one of the men who came to the house almost often enough.

"He is absolutely to be depended upon, that's why," she said firmly.

"I think he is just right for it, Florence," put in Mrs. Wanning. "It's remarkable he should feel that he can give up the time; such a busy man. He must be very much interested in the movement."

Florence's lip curled drolly under her soup spoon. She shot an amused glance at her mother's dignity.

"Nothing doing," her keen eyes seemed to say.

Though Florence was nearly thirty and her sister a little beyond, there was, seriously, nothing doing. With so many charms and so much preparation, they never, as Florence vulgarly said, quite pulled it off. They had been rushed, time and again, and Mrs. Wanning had repeatedly steeled herself to bear the blow. But the young men went to follow a career in Mexico or the Philippines, or moved to Yonkers, and escaped without a mortal wound.

Roma turned graciously to her father.

"I met Mr. Lane at the Holland House today, where I was lunching with the Burtons, father. He asked about you, and when I told him you were not so well as usual, he said he would call you up. He wants to tell you about some doctor he discovered in Iowa, who cures everything with massage and hot water. It sounds freakish, but Mr. Lane is a very clever man, isn't he?"

"Very," assented Wanning.

"I should think he must be!" sighed Mrs. Wanning. "How in the world did he make all that money, Paul? He didn't seem especially promising years ago, when we used to see so much of them."

"Corporation business. He's attorney for the P. L. and G.," murmured her husband.

"What a pile he must have!" Florence watched the old negro's slow movements with restless eyes. "Here is Jenny, a Contessa, with a glorious palace in Genoa that her father must have bought her. Surely Aldrini had nothing. Have you seen the baby count's pictures, Roma? They're very cunning. I should think you'd go to Genoa and visit Jenny."

"We must arrange that, Roma. It's such an opportunity." Though Mrs. Wanning addressed her daughter, she looked at her husband. "You would get on so well among their friends. When Count Aldrini was here you spoke Italian much better than poor Jenny. I remember when we entertained him, he could scarcely say anything to her at all.

Florence tried to call up an answering flicker of amusement upon her sister's calm, well-bred face. She thought her mother was rather outdoing herself tonight,—since Aldrini had at least managed to say the one important thing to Jenny, somehow, somewhere. Jenny Lane had been Roma's friend and schoolmate, and the Count was an ephemeral hope in Orange. Mrs. Wanning was one of the first matrons to declare that she had no prejudices against foreigners, and at the dinners that were given for the Count, Roma was always put next him to act as interpreter.

Roma again turned to her father.

"If I were you, dear, I would let Mr. Lane tell me about his doctor. New discoveries are often made by queer people."

Roma's voice was low and sympathetic; she never lost her dignity.

Florence asked if she might have her coffee in her room, while she dashed off a note, and she ran upstairs humming "Bright Lights" and wondering how she was going to stand her family until the summer scattering. Why could Roma never throw off her elegant reserve and call things by their names? She sometimes thought she might like her sister, if she would only come out in the open and howl about her disappointments.

Roma, drinking her coffee deliberately, asked her father if they might have the car early, as they wanted to pick up Mr. Allen and Mr. Rydberg on their way to rehearsal.

Wanning said certainly. Heaven knew he was not stingy about his car, though he could never quite forget that in his day it was the young men who used to call for the girls when they went to rehearsals.

"You are going with us, Mother?" Roma asked as they rose.

"I think so, dear. Your father will want to go to bed early, and I shall sleep better if I go out. I am going to town to-morrow to pour tea for Harold. We must get him some new silver, Paul. I am quite ashamed of his spoons."

Harold, the only son, was a playwright—as yet "unproduced"—and he had a studio in Washington Square.

A half-hour later, Wanning was alone in his library. He would not permit himself to feel aggrieved. What was more commendable than a mother's interest in her children's pleasures? Moreover, it was his wife's way of following things up, of never letting the grass grow under her feet, that had helped to push him along in the world. She was more ambitious than he,—that had been good for him. He was naturally indolent, and Julia's childlike desire to possess material objects, to buy what other people were buying, had been the spur that made him go after business. It had, moreover, made his house the attractive place he believed it to be.

"Suppose," his wife sometimes said to him when the bills came in from Céleste or Mme. Blanche, "suppose you had homely daughters; how would you like that?"

He wouldn't have liked it. When he went anywhere with his three ladies, Wanning always felt very well done by. He had no complaint to make about them, or about anything. That was why it seemed so unreasonable— He felt along his back incredulously with his hand. Harold, of course, was a trial; but among all his business friends, he knew scarcely one who had a promising boy.

The house was so still that Wanning could hear a faint, metallic tinkle from the butler's pantry. Old Sam was washing up the silver, which he put away himself every night.

Wanning rose and walked aimlessly down the hall and out through the dining-room.

"Any Apollinaris on ice, Sam? I'm not feeling very well tonight."

The old colored man dried his hands.

"Yessah, Mistah Wanning. Have a little rye with it, sah?"

"No, thank you, Sam. That's one of the things I can't do any more. I've been to see a big doctor in the city, and he tells me there's something seriously wrong with me. My kidneys have sort of gone back on me."

It was a satisfaction to Wanning to name the organ that had betrayed him, while all the rest of him was so sound.

Sam was immediately interested. He shook his grizzled head and looked full of wisdom.

"Don't seem like a gen'leman of such a temperate life ought to have anything wrong thar, sah."

"No, it doesn't, does it?"

Wanning leaned against the china closet and talked to Sam for nearly half an hour. The specialist who condemned him hadn't seemed half so much interested. There was not a detail about the examination and the laboratory tests in which Sam did not show the deepest concern. He kept asking Wanning if he could remember "straining himself" when he was a young man.

"I've knowed a strain like that to sleep in a man for yeahs and yeahs, and then come back on him, 'deed I have," he said, mysteriously. "An' again, it might be you got a floatin' kidney, sah. Aftah dey once teah loose, dey sometimes don't make no trouble for quite a while."

When Wanning went to his room he did not go to bed. He sat up until he heard the voices of his wife and daughters in the hall below. His own bed somehow frightened him. In all the years he had lived in this house he had never before looked about his room, at that bed, with the thought that he might one day be trapped there, and might not get out again. He had been ill, of course, but his room had seemed a particularly pleasant place for a sick man; sunlight, flowers,—agreeable, well-dressed women coming in and out.

Now there was something sinister about the bed itself, about its position, and its relation to the rest of the furniture.

II

—————

The next morning, on his way downtown, Wanning got off the subway train at Astor Place and walked over to Washington Square. He climbed three flights of stairs and knocked at his son's studio. Harold, dressed, with his stick and gloves in his hand, opened the door. He was just going over to the Brevoort for breakfast. He greeted his father with the cordial familiarity practised by all the "boys" of his set, clapped him on the shoulder and said in his light, tonsilitis voice:

"Come in, Governor, how delightful! I haven't had a call from you in a long time."

He threw his hat and gloves on the writing table. He was a perfect gentleman, even with his father.

Florence said the matter with Harold was that he had heard people say he looked like Byron, and stood for it.

What Harold would stand for in such matters was, indeed, the best definition of him. When he read his play "The Street Walker" in drawing rooms and one lady told him it had the poetic symbolism of Tchekhov, and another said that it suggested the biting realism of Brieux, he never, in his most secret thoughts, questioned the acumen of either lady. Harold's speech, even if you heard it in the next room and could not see him, told you that he had no sense of the absurd,—a throaty staccato, with never a downward inflection, trustfully striving to please.

"Just going out?" his father asked. "I won't keep you. Your mother told you I had a discouraging session with Seares?"

"So awfully sorry you've had this bother, Governor; just as sorry as I can be. No question about its coming out all right, but it's a downright nuisance, your having to diet and that sort of thing. And I suppose you ought to follow directions, just to make us all feel comfortable, oughtn't you?" Harold spoke with fluent sympathy.

Wanning sat down on the arm of a chair and shook his head. "Yes, they do recommend a diet, but they don't promise much from it."

Harold laughed precipitately. "Delicious! All doctors are, aren't they? So profound and oracular! The medicine-man; it's quite the same idea, you see; with tom-toms."

Wanning knew that Harold meant something subtle,—one of the subtleties which he said were only spoiled by being explained—so he came bluntly to one of the issues he had in mind.

"I would like to see you settled before I quit the harness, Harold."

Harold was absolutely tolerant.

He took out his cigarette case and burnished it with his handkerchief.

"I perfectly understand your point of view, dear Governor, but perhaps you don't altogether get mine. Isn't it so? I am settled. What you mean by being settled, would unsettle me, completely. I'm cut out for just such an existence as this; to live four floors up in an attic, get my own breakfast, and have a charwoman to do for me. I should be awfully bored with an establishment. I'm quite content with a little diggings like this."

Wanning's eyes fell. Somebody had to pay the rent of even such modest quarters as contented Harold, but to say so would be rude, and Harold himself was never rude. Wanning did not, this morning, feel equal to hearing a statement of his son's uncommercial ideals.

"I know," he said hastily. "But now we're up against hard facts, my boy. I did not want to alarm your mother, but I've had a time limit put on me, and it's not a very long one."

Harold threw away the cigarette he had just lighted in a burst of indignation.

"That's the sort of thing I consider criminal, Father, absolutely criminal! What doctor has a right to suggest such a thing? Seares himself may be knocked out tomorrow. What have laboratory tests got to do with a man's will to live? The force of that depends upon his entire personality, not on any organ or pair of organs."

Harold thrust his hands in his pockets and walked up and down, very much stirred. "Really, I have a very poor opinion of scientists. They ought to be made serve an apprenticeship in art, to get some conception of the power of human motives. Such brutality!"

Harold's plays dealt with the grimmest and most depressing matters, but he himself was always agreeable, and he insisted upon high cheerfulness as the correct tone of human intercourse.

Wanning rose and turned to go. There was, in Harold, simply no reality, to which one could break through. The young man took up his hat and gloves.

"Must you go? Let me step along with you to the sub. The walk will do me good."

Harold talked agreeably all the way to Astor Place. His father heard little of what he said, but he rather liked his company and his wish to be pleasant.

Wanning went to his club for luncheon, meaning to spend the afternoon with some of his friends who had retired from business and who read the papers there in the empty hours between two and seven. He got no satisfaction, however. When he tried to tell these men of his present predicament, they began to describe ills of their own in which he could not feel interested. Each one of them had a treacherous organ of which he spoke with animation, almost with pride, as if it were a crafty business competitor whom he was constantly outwitting. Each had a doctor, too, for whom he was ardently soliciting business. They wanted either to telephone their doctor and make an appointment for Wanning, or to take him then and there to the consulting room. When he did not accept these invitations, they lost interest in him and remembered engagements. He called a taxi and returned to the offices of McQuiston, Wade, and Wanning.

Settled at his desk, Wanning decided that he would not go home to dinner, but would stay at the office and dictate a long letter to an old college friend who lived in Wyoming. He could tell Douglas Brown things that he had not succeeded in getting to any one else. Brown, out in the Wind River mountains, couldn't defend himself, couldn't slap Wanning on the back and tell him to gather up the sunbeams.

He called up his house in Orange to say that he would not be home until late. Roma answered the telephone. He spoke mournfully, but she was not disturbed by it.

"Very well, Father. Don't get too tired," she said in her well modulated voice.

When Wanning was ready to dictate his letter, he looked out from his private office into the reception room and saw that his stenographer in her hat and gloves, and furs of the newest cut, was just leaving.

"Goodnight, Mr. Wanning," she said, drawing down her dotted veil.

Had there been important business letters to be got off on the night mail, he would have felt that he could detain her, but not for anything personal. Miss Doane was an expert legal stenographer, and she knew her value. The slightest delay in dispatching office business annoyed her. Letters that were not signed until the next morning awoke her deepest contempt. She was scrupulous in professional etiquette, and Wanning felt that their relations, though pleasant, were scarcely cordial.

As Miss Doane's trim figure disappeared through the outer door, little Annie Wooley, the copyist, came in from the stenographers' room. Her hat was pinned over one ear, and she was scrambling into her coat as she came, holding her gloves in her teeth and her battered handbag in the fist that was already through a sleeve.

"Annie, I wanted to dictate a letter. You were just leaving, weren't you?"

"Oh, I don't mind!" she answered cheerfully, and pulling off her old coat, threw it on a chair. "I'll get my book."

She followed him into his room and sat down by a table,—though she wrote with her book on her knee.

Wanning had several times kept her after office hours to take his private letters for him, and she had always been good-natured about it. On each occasion, when he gave her a dollar to get her dinner, she protested, laughing, and saying that she could never eat so much as that.

She seemed a happy sort of little creature, didn't pout when she was scolded, and giggled about her own mistakes in spelling. She was plump and undersized, always dodging under the elbows of taller people and clattering about on high heels, much run over. She had bright black eyes and fuzzy black hair in which, despite Miss Doane's reprimands, she often stuck her pencil. She was the girl who couldn't believe that Wanning was fifty, and he had liked her ever since he overheard that conversation.

Tilting back his chair—he never assumed this position when he dictated to Miss Doane—Wanning began: "To Mr. D. E. Brown, South Forks, Wyoming."

He shaded his eyes with his hand and talked off a long letter to this man who would be sorry that his mortal frame was breaking up. He recalled to him certain fine months they had spent together on the Wind River when they were young men, and said he sometimes wished that like D. E. Brown, he had claimed his freedom in a big country where the wheels did not grind a man as hard as they did in New York. He had spent all these years hustling about and getting ready to live the way he wanted to live, and now he had a puncture the doctors couldn't mend. What was the use of it?

Wanning's thoughts were fixed on the trout streams and the great silver-firs in the canyons of the Wind River Mountains, when he was disturbed by a soft, repeated sniffling. He looked out between his fingers. Little Annie, carried away by his eloquence, was fairly panting to make dots and dashes fast enough, and she was sopping her eyes with an unpresentable, end-of-the-day handkerchief.

Wanning rambled on in his dictation. Why was she crying? What did it matter to her? He was a man who said good-morning to her, who sometimes took an hour of the precious few she had left at the end of the day and then complained about her bad spelling. When the letter was finished, he handed her a new two dollar bill.

"I haven't got any change tonight; and anyhow, I'd like you to eat a whole lot. I'm on a diet, and I want to see everybody else eat."

Annie tucked her notebook under her arm and stood looking at the bill which she had not taken up from the table.

"I don't like to be paid for taking letters to your friends, Mr. Wanning," she said impulsively. "I can run personal letters off between times. It ain't as if I needed the money," she added carelessly.

"Get along with you! Anybody who is eighteen years old and has a sweet tooth needs money, all they can get."

Annie giggled and darted out with the bill in her hand.

Wanning strolled aimlessly after her into the reception room.

"Let me have that letter before lunch tomorrow, please, and be sure that nobody sees it." He stopped and frowned. "I don't look very sick, do I?"

"I should say you don't!" Annie got her coat on after considerable tugging. "Why don't you call in a specialist? My mother called a specialist for my father before he died."

"Oh, is your father dead?"

"I should say he is! He was a painter by trade, and he fell off a seventy-foot stack into the East River. Mother couldn't get anything out of the company, because he wasn't buckled. He lingered for four months, so I know all about taking care of sick people. I was attending business college then, and sick as he was, he used to give me dictation for practise. He made us all go into professions; the girls, too. He didn't like us to just run."

Wanning would have liked to keep Annie and hear more about her family, but it was nearly seven o'clock, and he knew he ought, in mercy, to let her go. She was the only person to whom he had talked about his illness who had been frank and honest with him, who had looked at him with eyes that concealed nothing. When he broke the news of his condition to his partners that morning, they shut him off as if he were uttering indecent ravings. All day they had met him with a hurried, abstracted manner. McQuiston and Wade went out to lunch together, and he knew what they were thinking, perhaps talking, about. Wanning had brought into the firm valuable business, but he was less enterprising than either of his partners.

III

In the early summer Wanning's family scattered. Roma swallowed her pride and sailed for Genoa to visit the Contessa Jenny. Harold went to Cornish to be in an artistic atmosphere. Mrs. Wanning and Florence took a cottage at York Harbor where Wanning was supposed to join them whenever he could get away from town. He did not often get away. He felt most at ease among his accustomed surroundings. He kept his car in the city and went back and forth from his office to the club where he was living. Old Sam, his butler, came in from Orange every night to put his clothes in order and make him comfortable.

Wanning began to feel that he would not tire of his office in a hundred years. Although he did very little work, it was pleasant to go down town every morning when the streets were crowded, the sky clear, and the sunshine bright. From the windows of his private office he could see the harbor and watch the ocean liners come down the North River and go out to sea.

While he read his mail, he often looked out and wondered why he had been so long indifferent to that extraordinary scene of human activity and hopefulness. How had a short-lived race of beings the energy and courage valiantly to begin enterprises which they could follow for only a few years; to throw up towers and build sea-monsters and found great businesses, when the frailest of the materials with which they worked, the paper upon which they wrote, the ink upon their pens, had more permanence in this world than they? All this material rubbish lasted. The linen clothing and cosmetics of the Egyptians had lasted. It was only the human flame that certainly, certainly went out. Other things had a fighting chance; they might meet with mishap and be destroyed, they might not. But the human creature who gathered and shaped and hoarded and foolishly loved these things, he had no chance—absolutely none. Wanning's cane, his hat, his top-coat, might go from beggar to beggar and knock about in this world for another fifty years or so; but not he.

In the late afternoon he never hurried to leave his office now. Wonderful sunsets burned over the North River, wonderful stars trembled up among the towers; more wonderful than anything he could hurry away to. One of his windows looked directly down upon the spire of Old Trinity, with the green churchyard and the pale sycamores far below. Wanning often dropped into the church when he was going out to lunch; not because he was trying to make his peace with Heaven, but because the church was old and restful and familiar, because it and its gravestones had sat in the same place for a long while. He bought flowers from the street boys and kept them on his desk, which his partners thought strange behavior, and which Miss Doane considered a sign that he was failing.

But there were graver things than bouquets for Miss Doane and the senior partner to ponder over.

The senior partner, McQuiston, in spite of his silvery hair and mustache and his important church connections, had rich natural taste for scandal.—After Mr. Wade went away for his vacation, in May, Wanning took Annie Wooley out of the copying room, put her at a desk in his private office, and raised her pay to eighteen dollars a week, explaining to McQuiston that for the summer months he would need a secretary. This explanation satisfied neither McQuiston nor Miss Doane.

Annie was also paid for overtime, and although Wanning attended to very little of the office business now, there was a great deal of overtime. Miss Doane was, of course, "above" questioning a chit like Annie; but what was he doing with his time and his new secretary, she wanted to know?

If anyone had told her that Wanning was writing a book, she would have said bitterly that it was just like him. In his youth Wanning had hankered for the pen. When he studied law, he had intended to combine that profession with some tempting form of authorship. Had he remained a bachelor, he would have been an unenterprising literary lawyer to the end of his days. It was his wife's restlessness and her practical turn of mind that had made him a money-getter. His illness seemed to bring back to him the illusions with which he left college.

As soon as his family were out of the way and he shut up the Orange house, he began to dictate his autobiography to Annie Wooley. It was not only the story of his life, but an expression of all his theories and opinions, and a commentary on the fifty years of events which he could remember.

Fortunately, he was able to take great interest in this undertaking. He had the happiest convictions about the clear-cut style he was developing and his increasing felicity in phrasing. He meant to publish the work handsomely, at his own expense and under his own name. He rather enjoyed the thought of how greatly disturbed Harold would be. He and Harold differed in their estimates of books. All the solid works which made up Wanning's library, Harold considered beneath contempt. Anybody, he said, could do that sort of thing.

When Wanning could not sleep at night, he turned on the light beside his bed and made notes on the chapter he meant to dictate the next day.

When he returned to the office after lunch, he gave instructions that he was not to be interrupted by telephone calls, and shut himself up with his secretary.

After he had opened all the windows and taken off his coat, he fell to dictating. He found it a delightful occupation, the solace of each day. Often he had sudden fits of tiredness; then he would lie down on the leather sofa and drop asleep, while Annie read "The Leopard's Spots" until he awoke.

Like many another business man Wanning had relied so long on stenographers that the operation of writing with a pen had become laborious to him. When he undertook it, he wanted to cut everything short. But walking up and down his private office, with the strong afternoon sun pouring in at his windows, a fresh air stirring, all the people and boats moving restlessly down there, he could say things he wanted to say. It was like living his life over again.

He did not miss his wife or his daughters. He had become again the mild, contemplative youth he was in college, before he had a profession and a family to grind for, before the two needs which shape our destiny had made of him pretty much what they make of every man.

At five o'clock Wanning sometimes went out for a cup of tea and took Annie along. He felt dull and discouraged as soon as he was alone. So long as Annie was with him, he could keep a grip on his own thoughts. They talked about what he had just been dictating to her. She found that he liked to be questioned, and she tried to be greatly interested in it all.

After tea, they went back to the office. Occasionally Wanning lost track of time and kept Annie until it grew dark. He knew he had old McQuiston guessing, but he didn't care. One day the senior partner came to him with a reproving air.

"I am afraid Miss Doane is leaving us, Paul. She feels that Miss Wooley's promotion is irregular."

"How is that any business of hers, I'd like to know? She has all my legal work. She is always disagreeable enough about doing anything else."

McQuiston's puffy red face went a shade darker.

"Miss Doane has a certain professional pride; a strong feeling for office organization. She doesn't care to fill an equivocal position. I don't know that I blame her. She feels that there is something not quite regular about the confidence you seem to place in this inexperienced young woman."

Wanning pushed back his chair.

"I don't care a hang about Miss Doane's sense of propriety. I need a stenographer who will carry out my instructions. I've carried out Miss Doane's long enough. I've let that schoolma'am hector me for years. She can go when she pleases."

That night McQuiston wrote to his partner that things were in a bad way, and they would have to keep an eye on Wanning. He had been seen at the theatre with his new stenographer.

That was true. Wanning had several times taken Annie to the Palace on Saturday afternoon. When all his acquaintances were off motoring or playing golf, when the downtown offices and even the streets were deserted, it amused him to watch a foolish show with a delighted, cheerful little person beside him.

Beyond her generosity, Annie had no shining merits of character, but she had the gift of thinking well of everything, and wishing well. When she was there Wanning felt as if there were someone who cared whether this was a good or a bad day with him. Old Sam, too, was like that. While the old black man put him to bed and made him comfortable, Wanning could talk to him as he talked to little Annie. Even if he dwelt upon his illness, in plain terms, in detail, he did not feel as if he were imposing on them.

People like Sam and Annie admitted misfortune,—admitted it almost cheerfully. Annie and her family did not consider illness or any of its hard facts vulgar or indecent. It had its place in their scheme of life, as it had not in that of Wanning's friends.

Annie came out of a typical poor family of New York. Of

eight children, only four lived to grow up. In such families the stream of life is broad enough, but runs shallow. In the children, vitality is exhausted early. The roots do not go down into anything very strong. Illness and deaths and funerals, in her own family and in those of her friends, had come at frequent intervals in Annie's life. Since they had to be, she and her sisters made the best of them. There was something to be got out of funerals, even, if they were managed right. They kept people in touch with old friends who had moved up-town, and revived kindly feelings.

Annie had often given up things she wanted because there was sickness at home, and now she was patient with her boss. What he paid her for overtime work by no means made up to her what she lost.

Annie was not in the least thrifty, nor were any of her sisters. She had to make a living, but she was not interested in getting all she could for her time, or in laying up for the future. Girls like Annie know that the future is a very uncertain thing, and they feel no responsibility about it. The present is what they have—and it is all they have. If Annie missed a chance to go sailing with the plumber's son on Saturday afternoon, why, she missed it. As for the two dollars her boss gave her, she handed them over to her mother. Now that Annie was getting more money, one of her sisters quit a job she didn't like and was staying at home for a rest. That was all promotion meant to Annie.

The first time Annie's boss asked her to work on Saturday afternoon, she could not hide her disappointment. He suggested that they might knock off early and go to a show, or take a run in his car, but she grew tearful and said it would be hard to make her family understand. Wanning thought perhaps he could explain to her mother. He called his motor and took Annie home.

When his car stopped in front of the tenement house on Eighth Avenue, heads came popping out of the windows for six stories up, and all the neighbor women, in dressing sacks and wrappers, gazed down at the machine and at the couple alighting from it. A motor meant a wedding or the hospital.

The plumber's son, Willy Steen, came over from the corner saloon to see what was going on, and Annie introduced him at the doorstep.

Mrs. Wooley asked Wanning to come into the parlor and invited him to have a chair of ceremony between the folding bed and the piano.

Annie, nervous and tearful, escaped to the dining-room—the cheerful spot where the daughters visited with each other and with their friends. The parlor was a masked sleeping chamber and store room.

The plumber's son sat down on the sofa beside Mrs. Wooley, as if he were accustomed to share in the family councils. Mrs. Wooley waited expectant and kindly. She looked the sensible, hard-working woman that she was, and one could see she hadn't lived all her life on Eighth Avenue without learning a great deal.

Wanning explained to her that he was writing a book which he wanted to finish during the summer months when business was not so heavy. He was ill and could not work regularly. His secretary would have to take his dictation when he felt able to give it; must, in short, be a sort of companion to him. He would like to feel that she could go out in his car with him, or even to the theater, when he felt like it. It might have been better if he had engaged a young man for this work, but since he had begun it with Annie, he would like to keep her if her mother was willing.

Mrs. Wooley watched him with friendly, searching eyes. She glanced at Willy Steen, who, wise in such distinctions, had decided that there was nothing shady about Annie's boss. He nodded his sanction.

"I don't want my girl to conduct herself in any such way as will prejudice her, Mr. Wanning," she said thoughtfully. "If you've got daughters, you know how that is. You've been liberal with Annie, and it's a good position for her. It's right she should go to business every day, and I want her to do her work right, but I like to have her home after working hours. I always think a young girl's time is her own after business hours, and I try not to burden them when they come home. I'm willing she should do your work as suits you, if it's her wish; but I don't like to press her. The good times she misses now, it's not you nor me, sir, that can make them up to her. These young things has their feelings."

"Oh, I don't want to press her, either," Wanning said hastily. "I simply want to know that you understand the situation. I've made her a little present in my will as a recognition that she is doing more for me than she is paid for."

"That's something above me, sir. We'll hope there won't be no question of wills for many years yet," Mrs. Wooley spoke heartily. "I'm glad if my girl can be of any use to you, just so she don't prejudice herself."

The plumber's son rose as if the interview were over.

"It's all right, Mama Wooley, don't you worry," he said.

He picked up his canvas cap and turned to Wanning. "You see, Annie ain't the sort of girl that would want to be spotted circulating around with a monied party her folks didn't know all about. She'd lose friends by it."

After this conversation Annie felt a great deal happier. She was still shy and a trifle awkward with poor Wanning when they were outside the office building, and she missed the old freedom of her Saturday afternoons. But she did the best she could, and Willy Steen tried to make it up to her.

In Annie's absence he often came in of an afternoon to have a cup of tea and a sugar-bun with Mrs. Wooley and the daughter who was "resting." As they sat at the dining-room table, they discussed Annie's employer, his peculiarities, his health, and what he had told Mrs. Wooley about his will.

Mrs. Wooley said she sometimes felt afraid he might disinherit his children, as rich people often did, and make talk; but she hoped for the best. Whatever came to Annie, she prayed it might not be in the form of taxable property.

IV

Late in September Wanning grew suddenly worse. His family hurried home, and he was put to bed in his house in Orange. He kept asking the doctors when he could get back to the office, but he lived only eight days.

The morning after his father's funeral, Harold went to the office to consult Wanning's partners and to read the will.

Everything in the will was as it should be. There were no surprises except a codicil in the form of a letter to Mrs. Wanning, dated July 8th, requesting that out of the estate she should pay the sum of one thousand dollars to his stenographer, Annie Wooley, "in recognition of her faithful services."

"I thought Miss Doane was my father's stenographer," Harold exclaimed.

Alec McQuiston looked embarrassed and spoke in a low, guarded tone.

"She was, for years. But this spring,—" he hesitated.

McQuiston loved a scandal. He leaned across his desk toward Harold.

"This spring your father put this little girl, Miss Wooley, a copyist, utterly inexperienced, in Miss Doane's place. Miss Doane was indignant and left us. The change made comment here in the office. It was slightly—No, I will be frank with you, Harold, it was very irregular."

Harold also looked grave. "What could my father have meant by such a request as this to my mother?"

The silver haired senior partner flushed and spoke as if he were trying to break something gently.

"I don't understand it, my boy. But I think, indeed I prefer to think, that your father was not quite himself all this summer. A man like your father does not, in his right senses, find pleasure in the society of an ignorant, common little girl. He does not make a practise of keeping her at the office after hours, often until eight o'clock, or take her to restaurants and to the theater with him; not, at least, in a slanderous city like New York."

Harold flinched before McQuiston's meaning gaze and

turned aside in pained silence. He knew, as a dramatist, that there are dark chapters in all men's lives, and this but too clearly explained why his father had stayed in town all summer instead of joining his family.

McQuiston asked if he should ring for Annie Wooley.

Harold drew himself up. "No. Why should I see her? I prefer not to. But with your permission, Mr. McQuiston, I will take charge of this request to my mother. It could only give her pain, and might awaken doubts in her mind."

"We hardly know," murmured the senior partner, "where an investigation would lead us. Technically, of course, I cannot agree with you. But if, as one of the executors of the will, you wish to assume personal responsibility for this bequest, under the circumstances—irregularities beget irregularities."

"My first duty to my father," said Harold, "is to protect my mother."

That afternoon McQuiston called Annie Wooley into his private office and told her that her services would not be needed any longer, and that in lieu of notice the clerk would give her two weeks' salary.

"Can I call up here for references?" Annie asked.

"Certainly. But you had better ask for me, personally. You must know there has been some criticism of you here in the office, Miss Wooley."

"What about?" Annie asked boldly.

"Well, a young girl like you cannot render so much personal service to her employer as you did to Mr. Wanning without causing unfavorable comment. To be blunt with you, for your own good, my dear young lady, your services to your employer should terminate in the office, and at the close of office hours. Mr. Wanning was a very sick man and his judgment was at fault, but you should have known what a girl in your station can do and what she cannot do."

The vague discomfort of months flashed up in little Annie. She had no mind to stand by and be lectured without having a word to say for herself.

"Of course he was sick, poor man!" she burst out. "Not as anybody seemed much upset about it. I wouldn't have given up my half-holidays for anybody if they hadn't been sick, no matter what they paid me. There wasn't anything in it for me."

McQuiston raised his hand warningly.

"That will do, young lady. But when you get another place, remember this: it is never your duty to entertain or to provide amusement for your employer."

He gave Annie a look which she did not clearly understand, although she pronounced him a nasty old man as she hustled on her hat and jacket.

When Annie reached home she found Willy Steen sitting with her mother and sister at the dining-room table. This was the first day that Annie had gone to the office since Wanning's death, and her family awaited her return with suspense.

"Hello yourself," Annie called as she came in and threw her handbag into an empty armchair.

"You're off early, Annie," said her mother gravely. "Has the will been read?"

"I guess so. Yes, I know it has. Miss Wilson got it out of the safe for them. The son came in. He's a pill."

"Was nothing said to you, daughter?"

"Yes, a lot. Please give me some tea, mother." Annie felt that her swagger was failing.

"Don't tantalize us, Ann," her sister broke in. "Didn't you get anything?"

"I got the mit, all right. And some back talk from the old man that I'm awful sore about."

Annie dashed away the tears and gulped her tea.

Gradually her mother and Willy drew the story from her. Willy offered at once to go to the office building and take his stand outside the door and never leave it until he had punched old Mr. McQuiston's face. He rose as if to attend to it at once, but Mrs. Wooley drew him to his chair again and patted his arm.

"It would only start talk and get the girl in trouble, Willy. When it's lawyers, folks in our station is helpless. I certainly believed that man when he sat here; you heard him yourself. Such a gentleman as he looked."

Willy thumped his great fist, still in punching position, down on his knee.

"Never you be fooled again, Mama Wooley. You'll never get anything out of a rich guy that he ain't signed up in the courts for. Rich is tight. There's no exceptions."

Annie shook her head.

"I didn't want anything out of him. He was a nice, kind man, and he had his troubles, I guess. He wasn't tight."

"Still," said Mrs. Wooley sadly, "Mr. Wanning had no call to hold out promises. I hate to be disappointed in a gentleman. You've had confining work for some time, daughter; a rest will do you good."